In the Dark

Kerry climbed the creaky steps quickly in the dark, walked into his small room, ducking his head automatically beneath the low ceiling, and flung himself onto the bed with a loud sigh. He buried his head in his arm. He planned to lie there for a long while and feel sorry for himself.

But the phone rang.

He waited for Sean to pick it up.

A second ring.

Come on, Sean. Get off the couch and pick it up.

A third ring.

Kerry groaned and pulled himself up. He walked over to the low counter that served as his desk, and fumbled around in the dark for the phone.

"Hello." It was a girl's voice. "Is this Kerry?"

He cleared his throat. "Yes, it is."

"Hi, Kerry." It was the sexiest voice he had ever heard. "I'm your blind date."

Other Point paperbacks you will enjoy:

Weekend
by Christopher Pike

The Lure of the Dark
by Sarah Sargent

Anna to the Infinite Power
by Mildred Ames

Slumber Party
by Christopher Pike

The Karate Kid: Part II
by B. B. Hiller

The Silver Link, the Silken Tie
by Mildred Ames

point

R.L. Stine

SCHOLASTIC INC.
New York Toronto London Auckland Sydney

ISBN 0-590-43125-0

12 11 10 9 8 7 6 5 4 3 0 1 2 3 4/9

Printed in the U.S.A. 01

BLIND DATE

Chapter 1

At first, when Kerry heard the sound of the bone breaking, he thought it was his. He closed his eyes, gritted his teeth, and waited for the pain.

He took a deep breath and buried his face in the wet grass. Over the pounding in his ears, he could hear the singsong chant of the cheerleaders practicing at the other end of the stadium. "GIVE ME A P! GIVE ME AN A! GIVE ME AN N! . . ."

Give me a *break*, Kerry thought.

Then he realized the pain would not be his. *Someone else* was screaming in agony.

Someone underneath Kerry was screaming in agony.

Strong hands grabbed him by the shoulder pads and pulled him to his feet. Then someone gave him a hard shove from behind. "That was a cheap shot, Kerry."

He was shoved again. He spun away, confused, and stumbled to the ground beside the screaming player. The player's eyes were shut tight and his mouth was twisted into a wide O of pain. He was lying on his back, one knee up, one leg jutting out at an angle that legs normally don't jut out to.

This isn't happening, Kerry told himself, slapping both hands hard against the sides of his helmet. I didn't just break Sal Murdoch's leg. I couldn't. I refuse to believe this!

Kerry climbed to his feet, and someone shoved him again. "Get back, turkey. Haven't you done enough?"

Number 88, Wilson, swung a fist at Kerry. The punch missed. But the surprise of it sent Kerry sprawling backward and he fell over someone's outstretched cleat. "Sal was already down," Wilson screamed, standing over him. "You didn't need to jump on him."

"Break it up! Break it up!" Coach Stevens yelled, stepping between Kerry and Wilson.

"It was an accident," Kerry said. "I couldn't stop in time."

Wilson kicked the ground hard, sending the dirt flying onto Kerry's uniform.

"Wilson, I said knock it off!" Coach screamed, holding Wilson back, his small red hands pushing against the big fullback's shoulder pads.

Wilson ignored the little coach. "You were number two!" he screamed at Kerry. "This was your way to be number one!" He turned away in disgust.

"That's not true!" Kerry called after him, his voice cracking.

There was no way it could be true. How

could Kerry compete with Sal Murdoch? Sal was All-State his sophomore year. He had been picked by *Sports Illustrated* as the best high school quarterback in the country. He had already led the Panthers to one undefeated season and a state championship. Everyone expected him to do it again this year.

Kerry was an okay player for a small guy. But he wasn't really into football the way his teammates were. It was just a game, after all. He probably wouldn't have even tried out if his father hadn't insisted — and if Donald hadn't been one of the school's biggest stars.

Now, thanks to Kerry, Sal was lying on the ground with his leg in too many pieces, surrounded by cursing, angry teammates shaking their heads, slamming their helmets to the ground. And everyone believed that Kerry had deliberately done it to him to be the number one quarterback.

Kerry felt a hard tap on his left shoulder pad. He ducked, thinking he was about to be attacked again. But it was his good friend Josh Goodwin, the backup punter. "Looks like this may not exactly be your day," Josh said.

"It was an accident," Kerry said. "Why don't they believe me?"

"You have a dishonest face," Josh told him. Josh grinned, his little black eyes lighting up above his big, bulby nose. He looked just like the toucan on the Froot Loops box.

"Why'd you have to fall on Sal?" Josh asked. "Why couldn't you fall on someone else — a cheerleader, maybe. How about Linda Miles over there? I wouldn't mind falling on her!"

Kerry watched Coach Stevens running to the gym to call for an ambulance. "This is serious, Josh. What am I going to do?"

Josh shrugged. "I don't know. Take up tiddlywinks?"

"I'd probably fall on my opponent's thumb," Kerry said glumly. He shook his head and started toward the crowd of players around Sal.

But two players, O'Brien and Malick, guys he'd always been pretty friendly with, blocked his way. "Just go away, Hart," O'Brien said menacingly.

"It was an accident," Kerry insisted.

"You were your parents' accident!" Malick yelled.

"Take a walk, Hart," O'Brien said, giving him a hard shove on the chest pad. "You're not wanted here."

"You're history," Malick said. "You're dead meat!"

The next few minutes were a blur, a nightmare of angry voices, shoving, and threatening words. Why wouldn't anyone listen to him?

"What happened? What happened to Sal?" It was Sharon Spinner, Sal's girl friend, running ahead of the other cheerleaders.

"Kerry Hart broke Sal's leg," O'Brien told her.

Sharon screamed. She stopped right in front of Kerry. Her face seemed to be on fire, her normally perfect blonde hair flaring up like flames. "How could you? How *could* you?!" she screamed into Kerry's face.

"I didn't — " Kerry started, but he could see from her wild, frantic eyes that she wouldn't listen to him.

"What about his football scholarship?" Sharon yelled. "What about his career? How's he going to go to college now? How *could* you?"

She didn't wait for any reply from Kerry. She turned and started toward Sal. But she tripped over the edge of the tarp they had covered Sal with to keep him warm, and fell onto Sal's chest.

"Oh, my God!" she screamed. "He's dead! He's *dead!*"

Kerry gasped for air. Everything went white.

"No, he isn't," one of the players said. "Cool it, Sharon. He's just passed out, probably from shock."

Kerry took a deep breath. Colors began to come back.

"You've ruined his life! Ruined it!" Kerry realized that Sharon was screaming at him again. "All he ever cared about was football. Now he'll never get to play anywhere!"

"The ambulance is on its way," Coach Stevens called, running across the field from the gym, the whistle around his neck swinging from side to side, his paunch bouncing up and down beneath his gray sweat shirt as he ran. "Okay, men, go get dressed. This scrimmage is over."

"The *season* is over," a player muttered.

"Who said that?" Coach yelled, still trying to catch his breath from his run. A flash of anger crossed his face, but he quickly stifled it. "Never mind," he said, shaking his head. "Just go get dressed. And, Hart — wait in my office, okay?" He shot Kerry a disgusted look.

"Oh boy," Kerry said to Josh. "What do you think he's going to do?"

Josh shrugged. "He's probably not going to name you team captain."

Kerry's teammates began to jog slowly toward the locker room. Some of them pointed at him menacingly as they passed. "You're dead meat, Hart," someone repeated. Most of them wouldn't look at him.

Kerry started toward Coach's office at the side of the gym. The sun was lowering behind the hills, casting a wide shadow across the football field. Kerry shivered in the cool air. He realized he was soaking wet from sweat. As he reached the door to Coach's office, he saw the white and yellow ambulance, its siren wailing, pull into the school parking lot. He shivered again and went inside.

The small room had that odor unique to

coaches' offices, a combination of gym socks and rubbing alcohol. A silver football trophy that had been converted into a table lamp sat on the edge of Coach's cluttered desk, providing the only light. A football-shaped mirror, streaked with dust, hung on the wall beside the desk.

Kerry looked into the mirror and wiped some dirt off his cheek with his hand. He pushed back his wavy, brown hair and tried to flatten it into place.

Ever since a girl at the mall had stopped him to ask if he was Ralph Macchio, the guy from *The Karate Kid,* Kerry had taken more interest in his appearance. With his dark hair and clean, dark features, he looked a lot like Ralph Macchio, but without the openness or confidence the actor conveyed.

The back wall of the tiny office was covered with team photographs, one photo for each of the twenty years that Stevens had been Panther coach. Kerry walked up to the wall and stared at the teams at eye level, not really seeing anything, just a blur of gray faces. Suddenly one face came into focus.

"I see you. I know you're there," Kerry said aloud.

He was staring at Donald's face. Donald, arms around the players at either side of him, grinned out at Kerry. Donald the champ, Donald the star . . . wearing number 11.

Kerry looked down at his own jersey and frowned. Why had he also picked number 11?

Why did he pick his brother's old number? Because he tried to do *everything* that Donald did, to be everything that Donald was? Why was he wearing a football jersey at all? Just because Donald wore one?

He turned away from the photographs and took a seat in the folding chair in front of Coach's desk. He tried to force his mind to go blank. He concentrated on waiting.

About ten minutes later, the inner door opened, letting in a shaft of bright yellow light from the gym, startling Kerry awake. Coach walked in and nodded to Kerry without really looking at him. His face twitched nervously. His cheeks were bright pink. He began to pace back and forth in the tiny cubicle.

"How's Sal?" Kerry asked.

Coach stopped pacing. "Not good," he said, his forehead wrinkling. "I don't like the fact that he isn't conscious. It's probably just shock. But I don't like it at all."

"It really was an accident," Kerry began. He started to explain everything, but Coach raised his pudgy hand.

"Of course it was an accident," he said, finally looking at Kerry. "I'm not about to believe that one of my boys deliberately went out to injure another one of my boys. And I'm certainly not about to believe that about Donald's younger brother."

Donald again.

This time Kerry didn't mind. Let him talk

about Donald all he wants as long as he believes me, Kerry thought.

Coach began pacing again, his face twitching. This wasn't easy for him. He wasn't used to choosing his words carefully. "Kerry," he said, "I know you've had a lot of tragedy to live with in the past year or so. . . ."

Kerry was too startled to speak. No one ever talked about his tragedy. Not his dad, not his younger brother Sean, not Josh, or any of his other friends. So, hearing Coach mention it gave him a real jolt, started his heart pounding.

"That makes this even more difficult for me," Coach said, still pacing, three steps one way, three steps back. "You'll have to leave the team. You can't play for the Panthers."

"But it was an accident," Kerry protested.

"That doesn't matter. The other players think it was deliberate. They won't play with you as quarterback. Most of them want to knock your head off."

"But if I stay on the team and— "

Coach put his fists down on the edge of the desk and leaned forward, staring right into Kerry's eyes. "If you stay on the team, you'll only be a morale problem. I'm sorry, Kerry. That's it. It's over. Go clean out your locker."

Kerry sat staring at the back wall, the smiling black-and-white faces of past teams looking back at him. He tried to avoid Donald's picture, but his eyes stopped on it anyway. He jumped to his feet, nodded to

Coach, and walked to the door. "Now I have the unhappy job of calling Sal's parents," Coach said, as Kerry closed the door behind him.

It didn't take long to clean out his locker. When he came out of the gym, he found Josh waiting for him in the parking lot. "I thought you could use a lift home," Josh said.

"Do you have a car?" Kerry asked.

"No," Josh said. "But it's the thought that counts, right?"

They walked past the high school and up the tree-lined street. A sharp wind blew down from the hills, the first touch of autumn. The sun was a narrow, orange ribbon outlining the low, sloping hills. They walked through shades of gray toward Josh's house. It was two blocks from the school, a sprawling ranch house on a rolling, hedge-lined lawn. Kerry lived up in the hills in a modest, two-family tract house, part of a development that was never finished.

"I'll walk you to your house, then take the bus," Kerry said, adjusting the backpack on his shoulders.

"So what happened?" Josh asked. "Did you get a lecture on why you shouldn't break the quarterback's leg?"

"I got bounced," Kerry said flatly.

They walked in silence for a few moments. "How do you feel about it?" Josh asked.

"Dad isn't going to like it," Kerry replied.

"I didn't ask about your dad. How's your cousin Gladys going to feel about it? What's your Uncle Max going to say?"

Kerry didn't laugh. They walked awhile in silence.

They didn't see the car, a long, four-door Oldsmobile about ten years old, until it pulled up beside them. "Hey — Hart!" Kerry recognized O'Brien behind the wheel. There were a bunch of other kids in the car. "Hey — watch out, Hart!"

"Listen, O'Brien," Kerry yelled, angrier than he had thought. "It was just an accident. Coach says — "

"I wouldn't walk around this neighborhood after dark," a voice in the backseat called out. "There could be another accident. Know what I mean?"

Suddenly the back window was rolled down. Sharon Spinner stuck her head out. "You ruined his life! I'm going to pay you back!"

"Sharon — cool it," O'Brien called back to her.

She seemed totally out of control. "I'm going to pay you back, Kerry!" A soda can came flying out of the back window. It bounced against Kerry's backpack, spilling soda down his jacket. The car sped off.

"Nice guys," Josh said.

Kerry shrugged. "Catch you tomorrow," he said wearily. "Thanks for trying to cheer me up." He hurried toward the bus stop across the street.

"I've got one last piece of advice," Josh called after him.

"Don't say, 'Break a leg!'" Kerry said without looking back.

"Aw, we've been friends too long," Josh said. "You know all my lines." He turned and headed up the smooth, curving driveway that led to his house.

The bus came a few minutes later, and Kerry rode in silence up into the low hills. At High Bluff Road, he stepped out into thick fog, cold and damp. Kerry shivered as he crossed the street to his house. The cold followed him right inside.

The house was dark except for a small table lamp in the living room and the glare of the TV set. Sean was lying on the couch watching a *Brady Bunch* rerun.

At least I got one break, Kerry told himself. Dad isn't home yet.

He walked into the room and tossed his backpack onto an armchair. Sean didn't look up. "Dad working late?" Kerry asked.

"Uh-huh."

"For a change," Kerry said. His dad was seldom around these days. "Criminals don't work banker's hours," he would tell them. But Kerry knew that after hours he mainly just hung around the station house shooting the bull with the other cops.

"Did you eat?" Kerry asked.

"Huh-uh."

A conversation with Sean meant asking a lot of questions and hearing a lot of grunts and hums in reply. Kerry looked at his younger brother and shook his head. Sean was as blond as Kerry was dark. With his sharp jaw and spiky haircut, he imagined that he looked just like Sting. But he was short and had a lot of pimples, which ruined the effect.

"A bowl of potato chips and a beer? Is that any kind of dinner?" Kerry asked, realizing that he was beginning to sound like a parent.

"Uh-huh."

Sean seemed to spend more and more time staring at the TV. Who could blame him? Kerry thought. At least in *The Brady Bunch,* they keep all the lights on in the house. And the family is together. And they like each other.

Kerry tried to remember the last time he'd heard from his mom. It had been at least a month. She had moved out soon after . . . soon after Donald left. She just couldn't take it, Kerry guessed. He still couldn't believe his parents were divorced. Sometimes he thought he heard her voice in another room. Sometimes he smelled her perfume.

Her weekly phone calls had become monthly calls. He and Sean were supposed to spend a month with her during the summer. But she had just started a new job, and the visit was postponed until Christmas. "I know you understand," she had said to Kerry over the phone.

But he didn't, really.

"I'm going upstairs," Kerry said. The laugh track on *The Brady Bunch* went wild.

"Uh-huh," Sean replied, his mouth full of potato chips.

Kerry climbed the creaky steps quickly in the dark, walked into his small room, ducking his head automatically beneath the low ceiling, and flung himself onto the bed with a loud sigh. He buried his head in his arm. He planned to lie there for a long while and feel sorry for himself.

But the phone rang.

He waited for Sean to pick it up.

A second ring.

Come on, Sean. Get off the couch and pick it up.

A third ring.

Kerry groaned and pulled himself up. He walked over to the low counter that served as his desk, and fumbled around in the dark for the phone.

"Hello." It was a girl's voice. "Is this Kerry?"

He cleared his throat. "Yes, it is."

"Hi, Kerry." It was the sexiest voice he had ever heard. "I'm your blind date."

Chapter 2

"Is this a joke?"

It was the only thing Kerry could think of to say.

"I don't think so."

"Uh . . . just a minute." Kerry reached for the lamp switch, couldn't find it in the dark. "I want to turn on a light. I'm in the dark here."

"Oh, don't turn on the light, Kerry. Let's talk in the dark." Her voice was kittenish, a soft purr. Every word seemed like an invitation.

"Okay."

Way to go, Kerry. Sparkling wit. You're really impressing her!

"I understand you live up in the hills," she said breathily.

"Yeah. How'd you know that?"

"Oh, I know a lot about you, Kerry."

Wow! This is unreal!

"What's your name?" he asked.

"Guess." She laughed, a soft teasing laugh.

"Uh . . . you sound like a . . . Nadia."
"Nadia!" she exclaimed. "That's right."
"I'm right? I guessed it?"
"No. But I guess I do sound like a Nadia." She laughed again. Her laugh was driving him crazy. It was such a . . . *dirty* laugh.
"I guess you like to tease a lot," Kerry said, growing bolder.
"Well. . . ." She adopted a little girl's voice. "I don't always tease. Maybe you'll find that out."
Oh, wow!
Kerry didn't think he could *stand* much more of this.
"Do you go to Revere?" he asked.
"Not yet. My family just moved here last week. I guess I'll start next week. Will you show me around?"
Will I!
"Sure. Hey — who told you to call me? Who set this up?"
"You can guess that, too."
"Karen Ailers?"
"Ha ha. No. . . ."
"Was it Donna? Donna Mueller?"
"No. . . ."
"Hmm . . . I can't think of anyone else. . . . It wasn't Margo, was it?"
"Score one for you."
"But I haven't seen Margo since she moved. She goes to North now."
"Margo insisted that I call you. She said you were a great guy."
"Well . . . I *am!* Ha ha."

"She said you were modest, too."

They both laughed. His laugh sounded more nervous than hers. He was thinking about Margo. They had been pretty good friends. They went out a couple of times, but nothing much happened and they realized they should just stay friends. Then Margo's family moved to the other side of town. She started going to North. He hadn't heard from her in months. It was really nice of her to fix him up with a blind date.

"Well . . . uh . . . how about Saturday?" he asked, then immediately felt foolish. "I mean . . . do you want to go out?"

"I thought you'd never ask." She laughed that sexy laugh again. But this time it was cut short. "Oh listen, someone wants to use the phone. I'll give you my name and address. You don't have to guess it after all." She quickly rattled off her name and address. He wasn't sure he heard her right. Was her name Amanda? He started to ask her to repeat it, but she hurriedly whispered, "Pick me up at eight. Bye." And then before he could say anything, she added, "It's been nice spending time in the dark with you," and hung up.

Kerry sat there with the receiver in his hand. I think things are beginning to look up, he told himself with a pleased grin. Why did it sound as if she was calling from a pay phone? That was weird. . . . But of course, the whole thing was weird! What a voice! The way she said his name . . . that amazing laugh. . . .

He leaped out of his room and bounded down the steps two at a time. He had to tell someone about this call. Even Sean would appreciate it. "Sean — you won't believe this! What a fox!" He stopped at the entrance to the living room. "Oh, hi, Dad."

His father, still in uniform, nodded hello. He pushed the police cap back on his head, revealing more forehead. Before he lost most of his hair, Lt. Hart looked exactly like Sgt. Andy Renko on *Hill Street Blues*. At least, that's what the guys at the station house told him, and he eagerly believed it. Even though he wasn't from the South, he affected the slight Southern drawl and the easy, open-gaited manner of the TV cop.

Then he lost his hair, and his resemblance to the TV cop along with it. The guys at the station house still called him Renko because they saw him with his cap on. At home, though, with his bald head revealed, he dropped the down-home manner and the Southern speech. He seemed to his two sons gloomy and ill at ease. It was almost as if he only came to life when he had his police cap on.

"Beer and potato chips for dinner? Can't you look after your brother better than that?" That was his greeting to Kerry.

"I just got home," Kerry said, feeling his face redden. Why couldn't he ever talk to his dad without feeling embarrassed?

"You were upstairs talking on the phone, weren't you?"

"Yes. How come you're still in uniform?"

"I'm going back out. I just wanted to check in on you boys. Everything okay, Sean?"

"Uh-huh." Sean was watching an old *Gilligan's Island*.

"Dad, I have to talk to you — " Kerry began.

"There's some McDonalds hamburgers in the freezer," Lt. Hart said, his eyes on the TV screen. "Remember, I bought extra so you guys would have them. Just put 'em in the microwave. Fourteen years old and he's drinking beer for dinner. What next?"

"I got some bad news today," Kerry went on. He was determined to tell his dad about the fiasco on the football field. He wanted to get it over with. Maybe with his father in such a hurry to get out, there wouldn't be the usual scene.

"I could use a little bad news," Lt. Hart said bitterly. "Maybe I better sit down for this one."

"Yeah," Kerry said.

"Bring me a beer — if there's any left." Lt. Hart sat down on the folding chair by the front door. He groaned. His back was acting up again. Driving a patrol car eight hours a day wasn't exactly helping it.

Kerry brought him a can of beer from the refrigerator. He stood a few feet in front of his father and watched him pop the top off the can. He was trying to decide how to start his story. Was there a way to tell it so that his father wouldn't explode?

No. He decided there wasn't.

"I'm off the Panthers." That was a good way to start.

Lt. Hart finished a long sip of beer. Then he put the can on his lap and slowly looked into Kerry's troubled face. "Tell me that one again." He suddenly looked very old and very tired to Kerry. He wished he had some good news — some wonderful news — to tell him instead, news that would erase the wrinkles that ran down his cheeks and bring back that Renko smile.

"Coach Stevens asked me to leave the team. There was an accident."

"What kind of an accident?" He took another long sip of beer.

"I fell on Sal Murdoch. It really was an accident. I broke his leg. Some people thought I did it on purpose. You know, to get his position."

"Why'd you do it?"

"I *told* you, Dad. It was an accident." Why was he starting to whine?

"It was an accident and Stevens kicked you off the team?" His father glared at him with the same suspicious eye he'd give a mugger or a grocery store thief.

"He said I'd be a morale problem. Too many guys think I did it on purpose."

"A morale problem? Does that idiot forget the contributions this family has made to his team? Why, Donald was the greatest player the Panthers ever produced. Donald put the school on the map with his running, and he saved Stevens's job for him by getting that championship! Donald — "

"Dad — we're not talking about Donald!"

Kerry was the one to scream first. His father seemed surprised by his anger. He took another long drink from the beer can to hide it.

"Donald's younger brother belongs on the Panthers," he said finally. His expression was more bitter than angry. He actually looked hurt.

"Donald is gone, Dad. Coach Stevens doesn't care about Donald. All he cares about is that I broke his quarterback's leg and — "

"Could you two keep it down? I'm trying to watch TV!"

"Shut up, Sean!" Kerry screamed, feeling himself lose control.

"Don't talk to your brother like that. Donald never talked to you like that." Lt. Hart crushed the can in his hand and dropped it to the floor.

"Stop talking about Donald!"

"Stop yelling at me, Kerry. What am I supposed to say? You tell me you got kicked off the football team because of an accident, and I'm supposed to say don't worry about it?" He stood up and pulled down his cap.

"You're supposed to talk to ME. You're supposed to react to ME! You're not supposed to talk about Donald!" Kerry screamed.

"I've gotta go," Lt. Hart said, sneering.

"Okay, okay — you wanna talk about Donald?" Kerry's voice was filled with desperation. He knew he should stop right there, not say another word — but he couldn't. "Okay, fine. Tell me about Donald. Tell me what happened last year. Tell me why Donald is gone. Fill in the missing piece, Dad. Fill in the piece that dropped out of my memory, those days, those weeks. I've got a hole in my brain, Dad. A big hole. You want to talk about Donald? Come on. Talk. Tell me what I can't remember." He grabbed his father by the shoulders. "Tell me what my brain refuses to remember! Come on!"

Lt. Hart pulled out of Kerry's grasp. He made no attempt to comfort Kerry. Instead, he turned away. Facing the front door, he said quietly, "Stop it, Kerry. Stop it now, fella."

Kerry's hands coiled into fists. He felt ready to explode. "Turn around, Dad. Turn around. Look at me!"

His father shrugged his shoulders, the blue uniform wrinkling at the collar, and turned around slowly. "Stop torturing yourself about last year," he said without emotion. "Sometimes our brains know best. Sometimes our brains want to protect us. Don't try to remember what happened, Kerry. Just accept it."

Kerry fought to keep the tears from covering his eyes, but he couldn't keep them back. "I miss him," he blurted out. "I — miss — Donald — so — much."

Lt. Hart turned around quickly. "I'll be back late," he said, his voice shaky. He opened the front door. "Sorry," he said. "I'm real sorry." And he stepped out into the night.

"Why do you always want to upset Dad like that?" Sean asked from the couch.

Kerry stood at the door, watching as the headlights to the patrol car came on, cutting through the thick wisps of fog. Headlights. Kerry closed his eyes and still saw headlights. The image was jarring his memory. Headlights. Something stirred in his brain. Most of the last year was missing from his memory, wiped out by some sort of — tragedy. Headlights were a piece of the puzzle. He felt that. He knew it. But he couldn't go any further.

The patrol car turned around. The headlights pointed down the hill. The two red taillights grew smaller as his father headed down to town.

Kerry stared into the dark for a long time. Then he walked slowly back into the living room. Sean hadn't moved on the couch. *Gilligan's Island* had gone off, and now he was watching an old *Leave It to Beaver.*

"Gee, Dad, you're so smart," the Beaver was saying to his well-dressed, smiling father. "Tell Wally and me how we can be smart like you."

"Do you want a hamburger?" Kerry asked.

"Huh-huh," from Sean on the couch.

"Is that yes or no?"

"Uh-huh."

* * *

At one-thirty in the morning, Kerry was seated at his desk, the goose-necked desk lamp throwing an arc of dim, orange light onto his essay as he struggled to focus his eyes to finish it. "What I Didn't Do on My Summer Vacation." Mr. Shannon, Kerry's English teacher, thought of himself as a real ace. He thought this assignment was the cleverest thing that had ever been foisted on a class of high school juniors.

"Poor Shannon," Kerry said aloud, his voice hoarse from weariness. "He'll have to read twenty-six of these. I only have to read this one."

English was Kerry's best subject. He liked reading. He could lose himself in any kind of book. He liked science fiction best, though. Somehow he felt more at home in other worlds. Kerry liked to write, too. Sometimes in past years he would write long, long stories and send them to Donald when Donald was away at camp. Donald thought Kerry had real talent as a writer. The memory made Kerry smile. One more paragraph to write.

He looked at the clock. One-thirty-five. His father still wasn't home. He could hear Sean tossing about on his bed on the other side of the bedroom wall. Poor Sean. It was tough getting to sleep after lying on the couch for eight straight hours!

The phone rang, and he jumped.

Who would call at this hour?

Probably Josh, calling to see how he was doing. Josh was one of those people who never slept. He needed only two or three hours a night, that's all. Drove his parents nuts!

Kerry picked up the phone after the first ring. "Hello?" His voice had cobwebs in it.

"Sticks and stones can break *your* bones." It was a strange female voice, a phony voice. It sounded as if she was pinching her nose and talking.

"What? Who is this?" Kerry asked, his eyes blurring from tiredness and the dim desklight.

"Sticks and stones and broken bones," the voice said.

"Who is this?" The voice was raspy and distorted. He struggled to figure out who it was. "Sharon? Is that you?"

He remembered how Sharon looked in the car on the way to the hospital to see Sal. She looked wild, wild with anger, out of control. Was she calling him now to annoy him, to frighten him?

"Sharon, if that's you, this isn't funny."

The female voice at the other end laughed, a high-pitched, exaggerated laugh like a witch in a kids' TV show.

"Sharon, if we could just talk —"

"The toe bone's connected to the foot bone . . . the foot bone's connected to the ankle bone . . . the ankle bone's connected to the leg bone. . . ."

Click.

She hung up.

A chill went down Kerry's back. He

dropped the receiver. It clunked and bounced on the counter top. He grabbed at it, missed, then grabbed it tightly. His heart was pounding.

Just a stupid practical joke, he told himself.

But it was scary, just the same.

It was scary to be disliked.

Kerry had never exactly been popular — not popular the way Donald was popular — with friends and girl friends always surrounding him, following him wherever he went, filling the house with laughter and warmth. But he had never been disliked, either.

And the fact that Sharon, who had always been kind of friendly to him, now hated him enough to —

He decided to call her right back and put an end to this.

He searched through his drawer for the school phone directory, pulling papers out, tossing them on the floor. He found it on the very bottom. He was surprised to see that his fingers were trembling as he riffled through the pages, looking for Sharon's phone number.

He found the number, blinked a few times to clear his eyes, and dialed. It rang once. Twice. Three times.

"Come on, Sharon. You know it's me calling you back. Pick it up. Come on."

"Hello."

A man's voice. Her father.

"I was calling Sharon because — "

"Who is this?" he asked angrily. "Never mind! I don't care who this is! I don't want to know which idiot friend of my daughter's would call at this hour! Just don't ever do it again!"

He slammed the receiver down, producing a loud explosion in Kerry's right ear. Kerry nearly dropped the phone again, but replaced it with a trembling hand.

One paragraph to go. He had to get this stupid essay finished. He couldn't let them get to him. He *wouldn't*. . . .

Chapter 3

"Okay, here are the keys."

His father handed the car keys to him reluctantly. "Remember, give it plenty of gas when you're starting it — but don't flood it. The damned thing has been real hard to start lately."

Kerry took the keys and flipped them into his shirt pocket. "I'll be careful about it," he said.

"New shirt?"

"Yeah." Kerry couldn't believe that his father would notice. "It's sort of a rugby shirt. I got it at that shop at the mall."

"Well. . . ." His father looked him up and down, probably with the same expression he had when examining a suspect in a lineup. "Fancy new shirt, clean jeans, brushed your hair back to look like that movie star you think you look like. I'd say you have a heavy date tonight."

Kerry blushed. He wasn't used to so much attention from his dad. "It's a blind date, actually," he said uncomfortably. The new shirt itched. His stomach felt a little feathery.

"She'd *have* to be blind to go out with *you!*" Sean broke in, and then he threw himself down on the couch, laughing like a lunatic. He thought it was the funniest thing anyone had ever said.

"Is that the kinda jokes fourteen-year-olds make these days?" Lt. Hart asked, removing his cap to scratch the top of his head, unable to contain the smile that spread across his face.

"Shut up, Sean," Kerry called to his brother, who was still laughing like a hyena, slapping his knees and rolling around on the carpet. "G'night, Dad."

He walked out to the car, an '82 blue Mustang, and lowered himself behind the wheel. He pulled the keys out of his shirt pocket and stuck the right one into the ignition. Then he took a deep breath. He knew his dad would be listening. If the car didn't start right away, he'd come tearing out of the house, and Kerry would have to sit through another lecture on how to start the car without flooding it.

He pressed down on the gas pedal, once, twice. He turned the key. "Come on, car. Come on. Start up. Let me get away from here."

The car started right up. He could see his father standing in the doorway, a disappointed look on his face. Carefully, Kerry backed down the short drive, turned into Hillside Drive, and headed toward town.

It was a clear, crisp autumn night. The air was cold and clean. There'd probably be a frost later on. A good night for snuggling up with someone, he thought. Then he said her name aloud: "Amanda."

It was all wrong. It was too straight-laced, too old-fashioned, too pioneer-days-on-the-old-frontier. Amanda. He had only talked to her once, but he knew she wasn't an Amanda. She was a Nadia. Maybe he would call her that. She'd probably think it was funny.

At the bottom of the hill, Hillside Drive divided into two roads, one leading toward New Town where Paul Revere High was located, the other leading to the old section of the city, the original village. Amanda lived on Sycamore Street in the old village. Kerry remembered it as being one of the nicest streets in town, a broad street lined with stately old sycamore trees and even statelier old mansions.

Maybe she's rich as well as sexy, he told himself. He tried to picture — for the ten thousandth time — what she looked like. He had already decided on straight black hair flowing down below her waist, sort of a Crystal Gayle effect — but sexier. And he had decided on deep, green eyes and a small heart-shaped mouth with dark, dark lipstick. And of course she was built like crazy. But would she be wearing a sweater to emphasize her fabulous body? Or would she come on more casual and demure in a blouse buttoned up to her chin and some sort of preppy long skirt? He couldn't decide.

And of course, she probably wouldn't want to "go all the way" with him until *after* the movie. But he could understand that. He liked a girl with some of the old-fashioned values.

He and Josh had spent several hours discussing this blind date, the phone call, and every word she had said. They were in Josh's den, lying on the soft leather couches, gazing up at the ceiling. A Springsteen album was booming from the speakers recessed on either side of the bar. Josh made him repeat every part of the phone conversation at least six times. Then he would say, "Man, she's hot! She is *hot!*"

Then he'd ask him to repeat a different part of the conversation.

Since the entire talk had lasted about three minutes, there wasn't a whole lot to repeat, and Kerry found the conversation getting a little boring after about the eighth go-round. If only Josh could think of something else to say besides, "Man, she is hot!"

The fact that she was so hot was beginning to make Kerry a bit nervous. He had to admit he wasn't exactly Burt Reynolds. *Suave* and *sophisticated* weren't exactly the words that came to mind when people described him, even if he did look exactly like Ralph Macchio. True, he wasn't a complete nerd, either. Like everything in his life — like everything about him — Kerry was sort of in-between, not really one thing or the other.

"I got another call last night, too," Kerry said. He decided to tell Josh about the threatening, frightening call mainly to change the subject. He described the voice, the singsong way of talking that held such menace, and the repeated rhymes about bones.

"Oh, right," Josh said casually, getting up from the couch to change the compact disc on the stereo. "That was me."

"Sure it was," Kerry said sarcastically.

"No, really," Josh insisted. "Did I scare you? I did, didn't I!"

"Come off it, Josh."

"I'm going to audition for a part in one of those slasher movies. I figure if I can scare you, I'm ready to try out. I really want that part. You get to slash twenty coeds to pieces. It's cool."

Kerry found himself getting really annoyed. "Josh, someone is trying to frighten me, and all you can do is make jokes."

"So I *did* scare you!" Josh said, bulging his eyes and twisting his face to look like a mad fiend. "All right! You wanna come with me to help me buy a big butcher knife?"

"Forget it," Kerry said disgustedly. "Hey, how is Sal doing? Have you heard?"

"You don't want to know," Josh said, turning serious at last. "I heard he was still unconscious. The leg is a simple fracture. But the doctors are worried that he still isn't conscious."

"I feel terrible," Kerry said. And he really did.

Now it was Saturday night, nearly eight o'clock, and he was feeling nervous — nervous and itchy. Turning onto Sycamore Street, perhaps the fanciest street in town, the old Mustang seemed nervous, too. It choked and backfired and nearly stalled out. Cursing, he pressed the gas pedal down, and the engine smoothed out. He slowed the car down to read the house numbers. Street lights on tall poles cast wide beams of white light through the trees onto the wide lawns, but it was still hard to find the address signs among the tall hedges and manicured shrubs.

This neighborhood should look familiar, he thought. He had school friends who lived on Sycamore. He had visited in some of the immense, old houses with their tennis courts, their pools, their room after room of antique furniture you weren't allowed to sit on or play near. But in the dark silence of a cool autumn night, it all looked different. The old houses, carefully shrouded behind tall evergreens and walls of hedges, took on an aura of mystery. Leaves fluttered in the pale light of the street lamps, casting moving shadows that made the smooth lawns seem to churn and bubble as if alive.

It's definitely spooky, Kerry told himself. At least up in the hills, the houses are close together so you can always see some signs of life, people in their living rooms watching TV, lights. Here, only the shadows moved.

But why was he thinking such weird thoughts?

There was the house on the next corner. He was about to pick up Amanda. It's funny, the things you think about when you're nervous, he told himself. His throat felt suddenly dry. His new shirt still itched all down his back and around his neck.

He checked the number on the small wooden address sign again. His foot hit the brake harder than he had intended when he saw the house.

It was a mess!

Even in the light from the street lamps, Kerry could see that the hedges were wild and poked out in all directions. The grass hadn't been mowed in months. Tall weeds stretched up everywhere, and tree limbs cluttered the ground. A rotting wheelbarrow lay on its side near the driveway, which was cracked and rutted with patches of weeds growing up through the ruts.

I guess the previous owners didn't leave it in very good condition for Amanda and her family, Kerry told himself. He looked up to the house, which was in no better shape than the grounds. Two white columns stood on either side of the front doorway. But even from the street, Kerry could see that the columns were chipped and cracking, with the paint peeling off. To the left of the columns, a screened-in porch had already been boarded up even though the weather was still mild. Two of the windows on the ground floor appeared to be broken. Large strips of paper or tape had been used to cover the holes.

Kerry parked on the street. As he turned the key and pulled it from the ignition, he realized that his hands were cold and wet. He looked back up to the house. It was completely dark!

They must be in back, he told himself.

But wouldn't they leave a light on at the front entrance if they knew he was coming?

Maybe they were having trouble with the electricity.

Leaves crackled under his shoes as he walked up the driveway. A weed wrapped itself around his left leg, and he had to stop to disentangle himself. There was no car in the driveway. The wide garage door to the right of the house was half open. It was too dark to see inside the garage.

He walked quickly up the driveway and onto the stone path that led to the front entrance. Like everything else he saw, the path was cracked and crumbling. Vinelike weeds flourished in the cracks. He was out of breath when he reached the front stoop. He stood there for a moment, remembering Amanda's voice on the phone, catching his breath, looking back to the street at his car waiting beyond the overgrown, junk-strewn lawn.

What does she look like?

If she only looks *half* as good as her voice . . . wow!

A dog barked across the street. Kerry jumped. He had become accustomed to the silence, to the sound of the rustling wind and the dry, scrabbling dance of leaves and their shadows.

He pressed the doorbell.

He couldn't hear it ring inside the house.

The dog barked again.

"Mind your own business!" he called to it.

He pressed the bell again.

There were no sounds from inside the house. No sounds, no lights.

He was standing in front of a large, empty wreck. Had someone played a joke on him?

He walked to the edge of the front stoop and leaned forward as far as he could, trying to see in the window. Drapes were drawn. He caught himself, regaining his balance just before toppling over the side of the stoop.

Maybe he should go around the back.

He pressed the doorbell again and kept his finger on it for at least half a minute.

This was silly, a waste of time.

There was no one in this house. No one lived here. From the looks of things, no one had lived here for more than a year.

Kerry kicked the door in disgust. "The best phone call of my life," he said angrily, "and it's all a joke."

Kerry turned and began to walk down the steps. And the front door slowly began to open.

Two faces peered out at him. Kerry hurried back up onto the stoop, tripping over a step. One dim bulb in the hallway behind the couple at the door provided the only light. It was a man and a woman. They weren't old, but they held themselves like old people. The woman had solid gray hair tied back severely from her forehead into a small, tight bun. She wore a knitted shawl around her shoulders. She was carrying a teacup and saucer in one hand. The man had a bald, speckled head. He was stooped over so that his head appeared to emerge from his chest. He wore square, frameless glasses. He was dressed in a blue bathrobe, which covered striped pajamas.

Kerry was so startled to see someone appear at the doorway that he just stared at them for several seconds. They didn't speak, either. They stared back at him. Their expressions revealed fear and surprise.

Finally, Kerry regained his senses. "Hi, is Amanda home?" he asked.

The man's eyes bulged behind the square eyeglasses. "What?"

"Is Amanda home? I'm her date."

The woman screamed and dropped her teacup. It shattered on the floor just inside the door. *"No! No! No!"* she screamed, her eyes rolling up to the ceiling.

The man didn't scream, but he seemed about to faint. He closed his eyes. His voice came out as a hoarse whisper. "Amanda is dead," he told Kerry.

Chapter 4

Kerry wasn't sure he had heard right. "Please?" he said.

"Amanda is dead!" The man was turning angry. "What do you want with us? What sort of prank is this?"

Kerry couldn't speak.

What sort of prank *was* it?

Suddenly, the woman stopped screaming. She stared at Kerry and grabbed her husband with both hands. "It's him!" she cried. "Look — it's *him!*"

They both seemed to recognize Kerry.

"What are you doing back here?" the man bellowed, struggling to free himself from his wife's grip. *"Why do you come to torture us?"*

"No! No! No!" the woman began screaming again.

Kerry turned and leaped off the stoop. He ran across the front lawn, stumbling over tree limbs, pulling himself through thick clumps of overgrown weeds.

He looked back over his shoulder. The man

had come out onto the stoop. Was he coming after Kerry?

Kerry reached into his trouser pocket as he ran and pulled out the car key. He had to get to the car. He had to get away from there. Gasping for breath, he reached the car and pulled open the door. He looked up to the house. The man had disappeared back inside. Was he calling the police? Had he gone to get a gun or something?

Kerry jammed the key into the ignition. It wouldn't fit.

Wrong key.

He dropped the keys on the floor of the car, fumbled around for them, and retrieved them. This time he carefully found the correct key before pushing it into the ignition.

He pumped the gas pedal once, twice. He turned the key. "Let's go. Let's go!" he said aloud, looking up to the house. There was no one on the stoop or in the doorway.

The car sputtered and stalled.

"Come on. Come on!" He turned the key again.

Again the engine tried but failed.

He pushed the gas pedal, then remembered he wasn't supposed to. He turned the key. Nothing.

He had flooded it.

Nothing to do but wait a few moments.

But did he have a few moments? He listened for a police siren. He looked back up to the house. Nothing happening.

The house . . . the house. . . .

There was a huge rec room in the basement. It had a Ping-Pong table, a billiards table — and a jukebox. Knotty pine paneling on one wall. Wallpaper with red and yellow balloons on another wall. . . .

How did he know that?

Had he really been here before? Did these horrified, sick-looking people really know him?

Who used to play in that rec room? Why could he remember the wallpaper but not any faces, any people?

Kerry felt a sudden surge of dizziness. It lasted only a second, just long enough to make him feel even worse, even more frightened.

That hole in his memory — it was so wide. Was this house one of the missing pieces? Who was Amanda? Why was she dead? Why didn't he remember her? Did he ever know her?

And the girl on the phone two nights before — had she sent him here as part of a cruel joke? Was she Amanda, too? Or had his leaky memory played a horrible trick on him?

He turned the key in the ignition and prayed. The car started right up. He put it into drive and floored the gas pedal. The tires squealed in protest as the car carried him away from the old house, past the silent sycamores bordering the street, past the hedges and the secrets that hid behind them.

He drove aimlessly around town, then up into the hills, past his house, up to Johnson's Point, which overlooked the entire valley and all the towns beyond it. He stopped the car about a foot from the cliff edge and turned off the ignition. There was no one around.

It started to rain, a few taps on the windshield at first, and then a steady shower. He turned off the headlights, scooted down in the seat, and stared at the water washing down the glass.

A few minutes later, the rain stopped. He stared at the tiny droplets of water, thousands of them that covered the windshield. Inside each droplet was a little reflection of moonlight. A thousand little moons.

It was a beautiful illusion.

Was this blind date an illusion, too? Had that girl with the sexy voice sent him back to an unwelcome place in his forgotten past? Another thought entered his mind, chilling him with its cruelty. Could the girl on the phone have been a friend of Sharon's? Was she helping Sharon to get back at him for breaking Sal's leg?

No.

No, he decided.

No, he told himself. And repeated it. No.

No, no, no.

He stared through the thousand tiny drops of light, and it all came very clear to him. He had played the trick on *himself*.

He had guided *himself* to that old house, a house that played some kind of role in his misplaced past. He had taken *himself* up that familiar path to that familiar front door.

The girl on the phone must have given

him a different address. It may not have even been on Sycamore Street. He realized suddenly that he hadn't written down the address she had given him so hurriedly over the phone. Why hadn't he written it down?

Well . . . for one thing, he was sitting in a dark room. But — he had felt no need to write down the address. His mind was determined to take him to the house where Amanda had lived.

Amanda.

Was that the name of the girl who called him? He was no longer sure. Perhaps it was a name his memory had wanted him to hear.

Kerry stared at the tiny water droplets. Suddenly they looked like car headlights to him, a thousand car headlights all coming toward him. He felt a stab of fear, a tug of memory. Then the lights all blurred together.

Kerry closed his eyes. He tried to hear her voice on the phone again, tried to recreate what she had said. Amanda. Amanda. Maybe she said another name, and he *heard* Amanda. Maybe she said another address, and he *heard* the address on Sycamore.

Those pale, sick people who opened the door of that dark house — they knew him. And they were terrified to see him again.

He pulled himself up in the seat.

Enough. This is too heavy, man.

And, wait a minute. . . .

What about the blind date? What about Amanda, or whatever her real name was?

She had to be home, wondering where the hell he was!

He had stood her up.

"It's been nice spending time in the dark with you," she had said in that sexy, teasing voice.

And he had stood her up! What a dork!

He started up the car and threw it into reverse. The tires slid in the mud from the rain, but he got it in control and got back onto the narrow road that wound down the hill.

Maybe she had called, wondering where he was.

If not — how would he find her? He didn't have her number. He didn't have her address. He wasn't even sure he had her right name. It wasn't going to be easy.

Oh — wait a minute. Of course, it would be easy.

He'd call Margo. Margo set up the blind date. He'd get all the info from Margo. Of course. Then all he'd have to do is call and explain why he had stood her up. And that *wouldn't* be so easy.

But he could do it. He had to. For one thing, Josh would never let him live it down if he didn't!

He pulled the car into the drive and ran into the house. All of the lights were on, but no one seemed to be around. "Sean! Hey — Sean!" The TV wasn't on. That meant Sean wasn't home. There were no phone messages for him on the pad by the phone.

So. Maybe she called and maybe she didn't.

He'd have to call Margo. Did he have her new number? No. He'd have to call Information.

"The Fremont family. Somewhere on the northside. No. I don't know the address. No. Yes — that's it!"

He started to push Margo's number, but then hesitated. It wasn't going to be so easy explaining to Margo what had happened. "Uh, Margo, thanks for fixing me up with a blind date. Could you tell me her address and her phone number? And what's her name? I didn't catch it the first time I spoke to her. You see, I was supposed to pick her up at eight tonight, but I went somewhere else instead."

Well, if he was ever *really* going to spend time in the dark with this girl, he'd just have to let Margo know what a jerk he was. He finished pushing her number.

It rang once. Twice. Three times.

He hung up after the eighth ring. There was no one home.

As soon as he put down the receiver, the phone rang.

He cleared his throat, then lifted the receiver to his ear. "Hello?"

"The ankle bone's connected to the foot bone . . . the foot bone's connected to the leg bone . . . the leg bone . . . the leg bone . . . *the leg bone. . . .*"

The shrill, nasal voice kept repeating the phrase over and over, growing louder each time, louder and angrier, until Kerry hung up.

Chapter 5

He was startled awake by the ringing phone. He shook his head, tried to focus his eyes in the bright morning light that invaded his room through the dust-coated window. Despite the cheeriness of the sunlight, his first feeling of the day was dread. The phone had become his enemy, and now it was summoning him before he was even awake.

"Sean — get the phone!" he yelled, his voice still hoarse from sleep.

But it rang and rang again.

He forced himself up from the tangled bedsheets, stubbed his toe against the leg of his counter, and grabbed the receiver.

"Hello, is this Kerry?"

It was the blind date!

"Yes. Hi." He tried to shake the pain from his stubbed toe, but it continued to throb.

"This is Mandy. Where were you last night?"

Mandy. Her name is Mandy. Why had he changed it to Amanda?

"I got the wrong address or something," he said, fumbling for an answer, knowing that he sounded like an idiot. "It's . . . uh . . . it's a long story. I'm really sorry. I felt terrible."

"I hope so," she said. Then she laughed. "I waited for you till about ten."

How could anyone sound so sexy so early in the morning?

"I tried to call you," he said, starting to wake up. "I've never done that before. Really. I mean, it's never happened to me before. I just — "

"I thought maybe you had car trouble or something," she said.

"I'm real glad you called," he told her. "I hope you're not angry. I — "

"Of *course* I am," she said. "I was looking forward to our date. After the big buildup Margo gave you. . . ."

He could feel his face turning red. He was glad she couldn't see him. Compliments of any kind embarrassed him. He knew he wasn't anything special. With that purring voice, a compliment was almost more than he could bear.

"I'd like to make it up to you," he said, forcing himself to be bold.

"I'd like you to," she whispered.

Wow!

"What's your address anyway? Now that I'm not talking to you in the dark, maybe I'll get it straight."

She giggled. "It's 42 Sizemore, near the old depot."

Sizemore! So close to Sycamore. But she must have said Sizemore over the phone that night.

"I'm sorry, Mandy. I just blew it. That's all," he said, still thinking about how he mixed up her name and her street. He shook his head as if trying to scatter the clouds that had fogged his memory. "Let's start all over again. I mean — "

"I'd like that," she said softly. "I have an idea. I'm starting at Revere tomorrow morning. Maybe you could meet me before school and show me around."

"Sure," he said, a bit more enthusiastically than he intended. "That's a great idea!"

"I hope you don't think I'm being too aggressive," she said, suddenly changing her tone.

"No, no. I like it," he blurted out. He felt his face turning hot and red again. Why did he feel so stupid talking to her? No one had ever made him feel this uncomfortable.

"Just because I'm coming on to you doesn't mean I'm an aggressive female," she said. She laughed, so he laughed, too. "Some boys get turned off by that," she added.

"Uh . . . you don't turn me off," he said.

What a master of understatement!

"That's the sweetest thing you ever said to me," she said. They laughed again. "I don't think of myself as aggressive," she went on, "but I don't always play by the rules, either."

What a *fox!*

There was silence for a few seconds. He simply couldn't think of anything to say. He was completely awake now. That's for sure. And he wasn't even noticing that his stubbed toe was still scarlet and throbbing. He was only aware of her voice, her whisper, her laugh, and how uncomfortable she was making him feel, and how he didn't mind feeling so uncomfortable.

"I have to get off," she said, breaking the silence. "But before I go, tell me one thing about yourself."

One thing. Think fast, Kerry. Man, he hated being put on the spot like this. One thing. . . .

"Well. . . ." He cleared his throat. "Some people tell me I look a lot like Ralph Macchio — you know, the guy in the movies."

Silence.

He could hear her steady breathing, but she didn't say anything.

"Uh . . . tell me one thing about yourself," he said, pleased with himself for thinking of it.

"Well. . . ."

It was her turn to think fast.

"Well . . . I'm really turned on by guys who look like Ralph Macchio," she whispered. "Bye."

"No — wait!" he practically screamed into

the phone. "Mandy — tomorrow morning before class — how will I know you?"

"Don't worry," she said. "I know you."

She hung up.

He realized he was soaking wet from perspiration. He pulled off his pajama shirt and flung it onto the bed. He started to pull open the window to allow some cool air in — and the phone rang again.

He smiled. "She just can't leave me alone," he said aloud.

He grabbed the phone. "Hi again."

"Sticks and stones will break *your* bones. Are you ready to die? Are you ready?" The nasal, rasping voice screamed into his ear, then hung up before he could reply.

Was it Sharon Spinner? The voice was too disguised, too distorted to tell. He put the receiver back on the phone, his hand shaking. Got to think about this calmly, he told himself.

He thought about Sharon. She was always such a Miss Perfect, leader of the cheerleading squad, homecoming queen, treasurer of the student council. She was always dressed in style, not too showy but just right, preppy and neat. She didn't seem to have the personality of someone who could make such threatening calls. She didn't really have much of a personality at all, Kerry decided. She was just a nice girl, pretty in a typical sort of way, friendly, but not terribly bright, or interesting, or. . . .

But she had threatened him in front of everyone. His mind flashed back to the chaotic scene on the practice field, with Sal lying on his back, his eyes closed, his leg stretched out at that weird angle, and Sharon kneeling over him, holding Sal's head in her hands, her cheerleading outfit all twisted, her hair flying all over her head.

He saw her angry face, saw the fear and disbelief in her eyes. "How could you?" she had screamed at Kerry. "You've ruined his life! How could you?"

And then later, in the backseat of the car O'Brien was driving, she had stuck her head out the window. Kerry saw again the wild look on her face, remembered the hatred with which she had spit out her words. "I'll pay you back, Kerry! I'll pay you back!"

It *had* to be Sharon, he decided.

Her life had been so neat and ordinary, so typical—until he had accidentally changed it all. He had invaded her safe, normal life. Maybe it was the first time someone had done that to her. And now she was striking back, paying him back with these ugly phone calls.

He picked up the phone. He had to talk to her. If she'd only let him explain what had really happened. . . .

He put the phone back. He decided to wait until he saw her in school. She'd never stay on the phone with him. Maybe if he could confront her, talk to her face to face, she'd listen.

He showered and dressed without really paying any attention to what he was doing. Faces appeared and faded in his mind. Sal, his face twisted in pain, then Sharon again, replaced by the sad couple at the house on Sycamore Street. He tried to shut them out, to think about Mandy. But he didn't have a face for her, didn't have an image to use to block out the faces he didn't want to see.

He clumped down the steps, walked through the dark living room to the kitchen, and found his father at the table, reading the newspaper. "Morning."

"Morning," Lt. Hart repeated without looking up.

"Where's Sean?"

"Sean?" His father peered over the top of the newspaper. "You don't really expect to see Sean before noon on a Sunday, do you?"

Kerry looked up at the kitchen clock, a brass frying pan with black numerals around the bottom. It wasn't quite ten. "I guess not," he said quietly.

"There's coffee on the stove," his father said.

"I'll just have some cereal." Kerry walked over to the cabinet and took down a bowl.

"Murdoch's still in a coma," his father said.

Kerry dropped the bowl. It clattered loudly on the counter top and dropped to the linoleum. "How do you know?"

"It's in the paper. Page one," his father said flatly.

"What?" Kerry was annoyed that his father had chosen to be so matter-of-fact about this. "Does it have my name? Does it say that I was the one who broke his leg?"

A long pause while his father finished what he was reading. "No."

"My name isn't in it?" Kerry fumbled around on the floor for the bowl, which kept evading his shaking hands.

"That's the least Stevens could do for you — keep your name out of it. Donald was his best player, remember?"

"Yes, I remember, Dad," Kerry said disgustedly, slamming the bowl on the counter. He practically tore the cabinet door off as he opened it to get the cereal box.

I haven't even had breakfast yet, and he's talking about Donald, Kerry thought.

"Want to see the article?" his dad asked, folding the paper to hand it to him.

"No," Kerry said angrily, more angrily than he had intended. "I was there, remember?"

"Don't yell at me," his father said, rubbing his eyes with the back of his hands. "You're angry at yourself — not at me."

"Just read me the headline," Kerry said, spilling cornflakes on the floor. "What does it say — 'Superstar Quarterback Ruined for Life by Bumbling Idiot Who Should Be Murdered'?"

"Yeah, something like that," his father said, actually grinning.

"Hey — don't tell me. I made you laugh," Kerry said in surprise.

"What d'you want me to do — cry?" his father replied, quickly changing the mood back to grim.

That was such a typical move by his father, Kerry thought. If a tiny human emotion happened to creep out, quick — cover it up. He decided he had won a small victory, anyway. He had actually made the old man smile, something he hadn't done in a long, long while.

"What about the headline?" Kerry asked, searching through the refrigerator for the milk carton. He finally saw it over on the sink where his father had left it.

"Read it yourself. I gotta get goin'," Lt. Hart said. He shoved the paper across the small kitchen table to Kerry.

Kerry shrugged and picked it up. "At least it's on the bottom of the page," he said.

"That's good," his father said. "Always look on the bright side."

The headline read: REVERE QUARTERBACK IN COMA AFTER BREAKING LEG.

Then a smaller headline read: SEASON OVER BEFORE IT BEGINS FOR PANTHERS.

Kerry crumpled up the paper and tossed it down on the table. His father finished the last drop of coffee in his mug and pushed himself up from the table. "Y'know, Donald would probably have — " He caught himself. He realized what he was doing. He stopped short. He pretended to cough.

"What?" Kerry asked testily, urging him on.

Go ahead — finish that sentence, Dad, he thought. Let's hear it. Let's hear what my fabulous brother would have done.

"Nothing," his father said, wiping his mouth with an already stained napkin. "I gotta go in this morning. Some idiots broke into the grainery last night, stole two dozen sacks of grain. Can you imagine?"

"What?" Kerry stared at his father. He hadn't heard a word. "Hey, can I ask you something? It's sort of about the law."

His father put on his police cap, working to arrange it in just the right spot on his head. "Sure. Hey — how was your date last night?"

"Uh . . . fine. Great," Kerry said, blushing.

"Listen, don't let your punk brother sleep all day, okay?"

"Yeah. Sure, Dad. But I'm going out. Josh and I are going to play a little one-on-one at the basketball courts behind school."

"Try not to break his leg," Lt. Hart said. He grinned again. "Sorry. Us cops have a sick sense of humor, I guess. It comes with the badge."

"Dad — my question."

"Shoot."

"Is it against the law — I mean, is it a crime to make weird phone calls? You know — call someone up and say weird things to them and threaten them?"

"You mean, make obscene threats?"

"No. Not obscene, really. Just threatening."

"Sure it's a crime," Lt. Hart said, giving Kerry the once-over. "Who are you planning to call?"

"Get serious," Kerry said. "It's this . . . uh . . . friend of mine. Someone keeps calling him and saying weird things to him. Do you think the police would — "

"Oh. A friend of yours," Lt. Hart said. "So it's just a teenage prank. Some kid with nothing better to do, huh. No. The police wouldn't take that seriously. Kids do that all the time. Listen, be sure to wake Sean up before you go, okay?"

"Yeah. Okay, Dad. See you later."

Lt. Hart was out the door before Kerry finished talking.

Kerry smiled. That was the best conversation he had had with the old man in . . . over a year.

He gulped down his cornflakes, then quickly washed the bowl out in the sink. "Just a teenage prank." His dad was right. He had to cool it. He had to stop letting the phone calls get to him like that. Sharon, or whoever it was, would get tired of it before long. Sure, it was upsetting, but what harm did it do, really? "Just a teenage prank." Kerry felt a little better. He grabbed his jacket and was out the door and halfway to the bus stop when he remembered he had forgotten to wake up Sean.

Lucky Sean, he thought, turning around and slowly walking back up the hill toward the house. The guy spends all his time vegging out, not a care in the world. He doesn't even seem to care about Donald being gone. Or if he does, he sure knows how to hide it.

He walked through the kitchen and living room and stopped at the foot of the stairs. "Hey, Sean! Sean! Wake up! Okay?" he yelled.

Silence.

"Sean! I know you hear me! Wake up! It's Christmas! Come down and see your toys!"

"Huh-huh," came the sleepy reply.

"In your face!" Josh cried, leaping over Kerry toward the basket, pushing the ball down to the hoop for a slam-dunk. The ball missed the hoop, missed the backboard, missed everything, and bounced away across the empty court.

"Nice shot, ace," Kerry yelled, chasing after the ball, which had rolled all the way to the tall, metal fence. "You're as good at roundball as you are with a football."

"At least I'm still on the team," Josh said. He grinned and crossed his eyes.

Only Josh could get away with a line like that, Kerry thought. But he still heaved the ball as hard as he could at Josh's stomach. Josh dodged away, hitting the asphalt, and the ball soared over him. "Nice pass," he said.

Kerry pulled a handkerchief out of his jeans pocket and wiped the sweat off his forehead. The basketball courts behind the school had to be the hottest place in the entire town. For some reason, the sun always beat down with a vengeance here, even when it was cool everywhere else, and the soft asphalt reflected up the heat.

Kerry didn't mind. It felt good to move and sweat. It was a beautiful, clear day, so clear you could see all the way to the top of the hills from the basketball court, one of those summer days that come in the middle of autumn and lull you into thinking that the winter cold will never arrive.

He and Josh played hard — and terribly. "You're supposed to hit the front of the backboard, not the back," he told Josh at one point.

"Now he tells me!" was Josh's reply.

They didn't talk much. The only sounds were the bouncing of the ball against the asphalt, the soft clip of their sneakers as they ran and scuffled, and the cries of some freshmen who had a game going on the far court.

"Here comes Dr. J!" Josh yelled, giving Kerry a body fake to the right and leaping left, sailing up to the basket, and forgetting to let go of the ball. He came down with the ball cradled in his arm, shrugged, and then froze.

"Hey — Hart! I almost forgot. Your blind date!" He let the ball roll away and slapped himself on the forehead. "What about it? How is she? How could I forget? How could *you* forget? Come on, man. Spill."

Kerry knew this moment was coming. He was surprised it had taken Josh so long to remember to ask about it. He went after the ball, scooped it up with one hand, and began dribbling around Josh.

"C'mon, Hart. How'd you make out?— forgive the pun."

"The date was . . . postponed," Kerry said. He tried to look mysterious. It wasn't going to be easy to pull this off, but he really didn't want to get into it with Josh. There was no way he wanted to tell him about the wrong address, the wrong name, and the couple that were so horrified to see him.

Kerry was certain that Josh knew something about . . . about the tragedy of the previous year. Most likely, Josh knew a lot more about it than Kerry did, since the entire year was nothing but a gap, a blank spot in Kerry's memory.

But they never talked about it.

Josh understood that it was something Kerry had to work out himself, in his own time.

The fact that Josh never mentioned anything about Donald or what had happened was one of the reasons the two of them had been able to remain close friends. Kerry knew he wouldn't feel comfortable with anyone who wanted to talk about all the things he didn't remember, or who wanted to help him remember.

"Postponed? You dork—you chickened out!"

"No, I didn't," Kerry protested, continuing to dribble in wider and wider circles around his friend. "It was postponed."

"Tell me another one." Josh made a stab at the ball and missed.

"I'm meeting her before school tomorrow morning to show her around," Kerry said.

"And you didn't go out with her last night even though every word she said cried out, 'Kerry, I'm hot for your bod!' "

"We just didn't get it together," Kerry said. Which was totally true. He pumped and sent up a lay-up. It hit the side of the hoop and ricocheted off.

"That's the whole story?" Josh still couldn't believe it. Kerry didn't blame him, but he'd just have to believe it. That was all he was going to get.

Josh started to dribble the ball, got his legs tangled, and fell on top of it. "Hey — I think I'm starting to get the hang of this game!" he said. "So she's starting at Revere tomorrow?"

"Yep," Kerry said, helping Josh up. "We had a long talk this morning."

"Did you mention me?"

"Of course not. Why would I mention you?" Kerry said.

"Why do you do anything?" Josh replied. "I can't believe you had a date all set up with this girl and you — "

He was interrupted by a boy's voice at the far end of the courts, yelling, "There he is!" Kerry and Josh looked up to see four guys running toward them. As they came closer, Kerry realized that all four of them were wearing yellow and black Panther sweat shirts. The guy in the lead was carrying a football under one arm.

"Hey — Bugner!" Josh yelled. "O'Brien! Thought you guys would be home reading the paper on Sunday morning. What happened? Did the funnies confuse you?"

Along with Bugner and O'Brien, Kerry recognized Malick and Henderson, all from the football team. Kerry felt his stomach knot up and his heart begin to pound. All four of them were running right toward him, determined — and ugly — looks on their faces.

Chapter 6

"We warned you to keep away from here, creep!" Malick yelled at Kerry. He took the football and heaved it. The ball bounced hard off Kerry's chest. He cried out, more in surprise than in pain.

"We're not bothering anyone," Kerry said, taking a step back.

"You're bothering *me*," Malick said. His red hair and freckled face usually made him look like a little boy. But now he was sneering, showing all of his teeth, his eyes narrowed menacingly, his big, freckled hands making and unmaking fists, and there was nothing cute or boyish about him.

"You're bothering me, too," Bugner said, trying to sound as tough as Malick and almost pulling it off.

"Don't be a copycat," Josh called to him.

Bugner raised a fist. "You keep out of this, Goodwin." He spat on the ground. "We don't have anything against you — except your choice of friends."

Kerry looked around for an escape route. He figured the wisest move here was to run. These former teammates hadn't come running up for a chat. He realized at once that he was trapped, surrounded on three sides by the high metal fence. The only exit was across two basketball courts. He'd never make it.

He looked up at the sun, white and pure in a cloudless blue sky, and he felt a strange surge of power. He made up his mind. He wasn't going to run from these guys. He suddenly felt as pure and strong as the white sun. He knew he was right. He knew what he had to do.

He would stand and fight them.

He looked down, the sun's glare still white in his eyes.

Malick came at him first. Kerry heaved the basketball at Malick's head. Malick ducked — right into Kerry's left fist. Malick's jaw made a crunching sound as it made contact with Kerry's powerful fist.

"Fists of steel!" Kerry yelled in a voice he'd never heard before.

Malick gasped in surprise and began to choke. He staggered toward the fence. Kerry ran after him, spun him around, and smashed his right fist into the other side of Malick's face. Malick dropped to the asphalt, choking and gasping for air.

"Hey, he's got *some* punch," he heard Bugner say to O'Brien.

"It was a lucky punch," O'Brien yelled, lunging at Kerry. Kerry dodged away quickly, turned, and landed a slashing karate chop on the back of O'Brien's neck. O'Brien's eyes nearly popped out of his head as he slumped helpless to the ground.

"He's tough, he's tough," O'Brien muttered over and over.

"You ain't seen nothin' yet!" Kerry cried. He ran over to O'Brien, scooped him up off the ground, and held him high over his head like a sack of flour. He felt another surge of power. His arms crackled with electricity. O'Brien felt light as a feather.

With a cry of triumph, Kerry tossed O'Brien onto the attacking Bugner and Henderson. They both yelped in pain and astonishment as the heavy body fell on top of them, sending them sprawling backward to the ground.

"Nice toss, ace!" Josh called from the sidelines.

"We give! We give! Please — stop!" pleaded Bugner and Henderson.

"Stop! Stop it!" another voice, a female voice, called from the far end of the tennis courts.

Bugner and Henderson struggled out from under O'Brien and scrambled to their feet. Groggily, O'Brien tried to sit up. Malick staggered to the fence and held himself up against it, still gasping in pain.

Everyone turned to watch the girl running

toward them, yelling, "Stop! Stop it right now!" It was Sharon Spinner, Sal's girl friend.

She ran up to Kerry and put a hand on his shoulder. It took her a few seconds to catch her breath. "What's going on? What are you doing?" she asked. She didn't wait for an answer. "Sal's fine. He just called me. He's going to be okay."

"That's great news!" Kerry cried happily.

"He told me to tell everyone it was an accident," Sharon said, her hand still resting on Kerry's shoulder. "It wasn't Kerry's fault. Sal said everyone has to know that."

There was a moment of surprised silence while everyone let her words — Sal's words — sink in.

"I guess I owe you an apology," Sharon said, looking down at the ground. "I guess we all do." She gave Kerry a quick, soft kiss on the cheek.

"Yeah. I guess we do," O'Brien said, climbing to his feet. He walked over and shook Kerry's hand.

"Sorry, Hart. No offense, man," Malick said, rubbing his broken jaw.

"Yeah. No offense, man," Bugner and Henderson echoed.

"Let's not talk about it anymore," Kerry said, feeling warm and happy. "Let's let bygones be bygones. Okay?" He smiled.

He looked up at the sun, white and pure. The pure, white light flowed through him. Still smiling, he looked down.

Sharon was gone, vanished into thin air.

He blinked. Blinked again. The four angry football players were coming toward him, ready to attack.

"What are you smiling about, you little puke?" Malick demanded. He wasn't injured anymore. None of them were. There had been no fight.

What a time to be daydreaming, Kerry thought.

But what a fantastic daydream!

The white glare of the sun still clouded his eyes, but he was back in the real world now.

"Sal's in the hospital — and you're smiling!" Malick said bitterly. He raised a big fist and took a step toward Kerry.

"Now, wait a minute, Malick!" Kerry bounced the basketball hard against the asphalt. "Sal will tell you it was an accident! Why can't you get that through your thick head?"

"Sal isn't here to tell us — is he, Hart?" O'Brien said. He pulled up the sleeves of his sweat shirt as if preparing to fight.

"Let's pause for a few moments of nonviolence," Josh said. Kerry could see that he was looking for an escape route, too, and coming to the same unpleasant realization that Kerry had. The freshmen on the next court had broken up their game. They were all leaning against the far fence, watching in silence.

O'Brien shoved Josh hard, then shoved him again. "Take a walk, beakface."

Josh looked as if he was going to say something, then thought better of it. He backed away. "Listen, there are witnesses here," he said finally. "You guys aren't going to get away with anything. You might as well — "

"Get away with what?" O'Brien demanded. "You mean get away with *this*?" He reached his arm back as if cocking a rifle, then shot it forward and gave Kerry a powerful, thrusting punch in the solar plexis. Kerry choked and dropped to his knees.

"What are you guys trying to prove? That you're neanderthals?" Josh cried, his voice rising a pitch or two. "Leave him alone!"

"Shut up, Goodwin," Bugner cried. He turned and pulled Kerry, who was still gasping for breath, to his feet. Then he swung a punch that just missed Kerry's right eye. Blood poured from the cut it opened on Kerry's cheek.

O'Brien grabbed Kerry by the shoulders as if propping him up into position. Then he slugged him hard in the mouth. Kerry's lip split. His face was covered with blood.

"Hey — that's enough," Malick cried, looking nervously toward the freshmen ballplayers, who were still leaning in silence against the far fence. "It was just an accident, Hart."

The four of them laughed heartily at this joke of Malick's.

"Hey — you hurt my hand with your face!" O'Brien yelled angrily, holding his right fist tenderly in his left hand. He wheeled around and drove his left fist deep into Kerry's stomach.

Kerry moaned and slumped to the ground, breathing noisily, blood pouring from his face.

"It was an accident!" Bugner repeated. "Just an accident!"

O'Brien pointed a threatening finger at Josh, who was standing unsteadily, white with fear, by the fence. "You'd better keep your big mouth shut, Goodwin. You never know when another accident might happen — do you?"

Josh was too upset to reply. He looked away.

The four football players slapped each other's hands as if they had just scored a winning touchdown. Then they trotted off together across the court, grim-faced but victorious.

Josh leaned against the fence, lowered his head, and had the dry heaves. It took a long time to get his stomach under control, and when he finally stopped heaving, he was too dizzy to walk. He took several deep breaths, felt a little better, and hurried over to help Kerry, who still lay choking on his own blood, his eyes closed, on the hot, steaming asphalt.

Chapter 7

He got to school early the next morning, before seven-thirty. There was no one waiting for him outside the building. He walked around to the side and looked up and down the parking lot. No one. So he went inside.

His footsteps echoed off the tile walls in the empty corridor. There was a girl standing beside his locker. She was tall and had very light blonde hair. She was wearing a plain blue dress, sort of a smock.

He walked up to her and tried to smile, but his swollen lips wouldn't cooperate. He saw that she had a ribbon in her hair, red and yellow hearts, the kind of ribbon a little girl would wear. Her eyes were pale blue, almost gray. They were translucent. They seemed to be painted on, like a doll's eyes.

Everything about her was light and pale — except for her lips. Her mouth was wide, pulled up in a wide grin, and she wore dark purple lipstick, which looked even darker and more out of place against her powder-white skin. He thought she looked a little like Alice in Wonderland, except for those purple lips.

"Hi, are you Mandy?" It was an effort to talk. Every word made his entire face hurt.

"Mandy?" She looked at him as if he were a piece of spoiled fish. "No. I'm Sarabeth Hoskins. Who are you?" Her dark lips formed a sneer.

He stood in stunned silence for a long moment. "Oh. Sorry."

Then she laughed, and he recognized the laugh. "I couldn't keep a straight face," she said, putting a hand on his shoulder. She gave his shoulder a little squeeze and dropped her hand. Her hands were tiny, he saw, like a doll's hands. "It's nice to meet you finally, Kerry." Her voice was softer and smaller than it had been on the phone.

"Yeah," he said, still feeling the squeeze of her hand on his shoulder. Such a strange thing to do, he thought.

"You look disgusting," she said, examining his face.

"I — uh — I fell out of bed this morning."

"Do you live on the edge of a cliff?" She laughed. He tried to laugh, but it made his stomach and his side ache with pain, so he cut it short. "Does it hurt?" she asked, her voice filling with sympathy.

"No, not much," he lied.

"Well, it's killing me! Ha ha!"

Where did that loud, dirty laugh come from? Kerry wondered. Her voice was so soft, so kittenish. He decided that her mouth belonged on a different face. But he liked her sense of humor.

"Please — don't make me laugh," he said, holding his side.

"I'm sorry," she said quickly, biting her lower lip. "I have a rotten sense of humor, I'm afraid."

He started to protest.

"But I have some very good qualities, too," she added. Her purple mouth formed a sly smile. It was very sexy, especially on that pale, innocent face.

Kerry tried to smile back, but it made the bruise on his cheek throb. He really was in bad shape. It was nearly impossible to drag himself out of bed, and for a few seconds, he had considered staying home, lying around for a day to try to heal. But he couldn't stand her up again. No way.

He had actually screamed when he tried to wash his face. The warm water burned like acid. But it was worth it. He was glad he had forced himself to come to school. He looked at Mandy, so pale, so paper pale in the dim corridor light, those flat blue eyes looking back at him. He decided she was beautiful — in an unusual sort of way.

"I want to apologize again for Saturday night," he said.

"Okay. Go ahead."

"I apologize."

"Very eloquent," she said. "Apology accepted. Now how about my tour? This school is bigger than I thought. How many kids go here?"

"I don't know."

"Well, I can see I'm going to learn a lot on this tour," she said, and she took his arm. Her little hand felt cold. Good — she must be nervous, too, Kerry told himself.

"Where shall we start?" he asked, a little uncomfortable with her holding on to him. "Whose homeroom are you in? Did they tell you?"

"Three-oh-two," she said.

"Hopewell. He's all right. He makes bad jokes about the morning announcements and laughs at his own jokes. But you don't have to listen. Here. I'll show you where three-oh-two is. Then I'll show you the cafeteria and the library."

A few early birds had begun to arrive. The silence of the halls was interrupted by the clanking of locker doors and the slam of books being dropped into them. Two girls Kerry didn't know walked by, giving them wide, openmouthed stares. Kerry decided they must make quite a sight — this tall blonde girl in the old-fashioned blue smock, and him with his head all red and puffed up like a salami.

"You just passed three-oh-two," she said, pulling on his arm.

"Oh. Sorry." He shook his head as if trying to get his brain to work. "I'm a little out of it this morning."

"Maybe we should just sit down somewhere," she suggested. "Like in the nurse's office."

"I'm okay," he said quickly. "Here's the cafeteria. No one eats here if they can help it. But sometimes you don't have a choice."

"Gee, it sure is green, isn't it," she said, squeezing his arm. "I don't think I've ever seen a room that green."

"It looks even greener after lunch," he said. He smiled. It didn't hurt that much. Maybe his face was loosening up. Or maybe she had a healing touch. "Where'd you go before here?" he asked.

The question seemed to surprise her. Her eyes grew wide for a second and her mouth formed a bright O. "I went to a private school . . . a very private school," she said, turning to watch a girl with pink hair and a fake leopard-skin jacket who walked by.

"Where?"

"What?" She seemed distracted.

"Where was the school?"

"In a very private place, of course." She laughed. "You wouldn't know it."

"Where are you from?"

"A lot of places. I've moved around a lot. Now I'm from here."

"Well, I can see I'm going to learn a lot on this tour!" he said.

She laughed and pulled herself closer to him, her dress rubbing against his side. "I like to be mysterious," she said in a mysterious, movie-spy sort of voice.

"You're very good at it," he told her.

"Compliments will get you everywhere," she said, pulling away from him and letting go of his arm. "Where are we?"

"That's the vice-principal's office," he said.

"What kind of vice does he offer?" She smiled at him, leaned close, and rested her head on his shoulder for just a second. It was a simple, innocent-seeming gesture, but it drove Kerry absolutely wild.

How will I ever be able to think about anything else but her? he asked himself, realizing that he was being captivated, that she had managed to completely win him over with just a few smiles and touches.

Was she doing it deliberately?

Kerry decided she was clinging to him so much because she was insecure. It wasn't easy to start at a new school — especially if you were used to a place that was very different. And Revere was about as far from an exclusive private school as you could get. Why, only about twenty percent of the kids who graduated went on to college, and most of them went to two-year colleges nearby. And, obviously, she had come from a place where kids dressed a lot more formally.

"You were in a fight — *weren't* you!" she said suddenly, almost accusingly.

"Yeah. I was almost in it," Kerry said, the memory of it rushing back, the crush of fists against his face, the gasping for air. He let out a small sigh.

"Do you often do such macho things?" she asked provocatively.

"Every day," he said sarcastically. "I like a good fight before breakfast. It wakes me up in the morning."

"You're not very good at sarcasm," she said, her dark lips frowning.

"I'm starting to get better at it," he said. He realized he was trying to be as mysterious as she was. "Look, Mandy, I really don't want to talk about it. There was a misunderstanding, and some guys here think I did something that I didn't. So they beat the crap out of me. It wasn't too macho or interesting or anything. I'll tell you the truth — it was the first fight I was ever in in my whole life. And I just hope that — "

"Is that the gym?" she interrupted. He realized that she hadn't heard a word he'd been saying. "Is there a boys' gym and a girls' gym?"

He scowled. He was hurt that she had gotten so easily distracted. What had happened to him was pretty dramatic, after all. She didn't have to smother him with sympathy — they had just met — but she could at least pretend to listen.

"No, there's only one gym," he told her. "Everything is coed here."

"I like that," she purred, sounding sexy again.

"There was a bond issue last year to add a swimming pool, but it was voted down. Everything having to do with Revere gets voted down." He opened the door and the familiar gym smell greeted them both.

She looked at her watch. He couldn't figure out if she was bored or just nervous about her first day. He decided she was nervous. "It's almost time for the bell," he said. "You can walk me back to my locker. It's near your homeroom."

She gave him a warm smile that spread across her face. They made their way through the crowded, noisy hallway that a few minutes before had been theirs alone.

"Hey, Hart — where'd you get the fat lip?"

He didn't see who was calling to him.

"Is that your face — or did you forget to take out the garbage?"

"You've got nice friends," Mandy said, yelling above the roar of shouting voices and slamming lockers.

"Everyone's a comedian," Kerry muttered.

"What?"

"Never mind."

They turned a corner and stopped next to his locker. "Your room is right over there, remember?" he said.

"It was so nice of you to come early and show me everything," she said, lowering her eyes. Then she grabbed his hand and shook it, her cold, little hand grasping his tightly, almost too tightly.

"I — uh — wanted to meet you," he said. "Listen, there's a — uh — dance here Sunday night, some sort of autumn dance or something."

"I'd love to," she said. She gave him the

warm, wide smile again. "I'll be your blind date one week late."

"Good deal," he said.

The hall was nearly empty. Most kids were in their homerooms.

"Do you think you'll be able to find the house this time?" she asked. "I'll tell you what — I'll meet you here at school." She didn't seem to want to leave. The thought that she wanted to stay with him made Kerry smile.

"Good idea," he said.

"Well . . . I guess I'll see you . . . " she said slowly.

She's beautiful, he thought. She's unusually beautiful.

He turned and opened his locker.

"Ohhh no!!" she screamed.

"I don't believe it!" he cried.

They both stared at the inside of his narrow locker, at the locker walls, at his notebooks and his textbooks — all smeared, all covered with blood.

She grabbed his arm and squeezed it tightly. She stared at him, her blue eyes filled with concern and confusion. "Kerry," she said in a trembling voice, "is someone out to *get* you?"

Chapter 8

The blood turned out to be red paint.

But that didn't make Kerry's day any easier.

First, he had to be excused from homeroom to go to the principal's office and see about getting new textbooks. The principal, Mr. Conquest, was normally a mild-mannered, almost wimpy sort of a guy who always wore ragged gray cardigans several sizes too large, and walked around with an unlit pipe in his mouth. But he became enraged when Kerry told him why he needed the new texts.

"This is not a practical joke," Conquest said, slamming the bowl of his pipe against his desk top dramatically. "This is an act of vandalism. I cannot tolerate wanton acts of violence on school property."

Kerry sat uncomfortably across from the principal's desk, his face aching and swollen, red paint on his hands. "Yeah, I agree," he said quietly. But when Conquest demanded to know if Kerry had any idea who might have poured the paint into his locker, Kerry just shrugged.

"What happened to your face?" Conquest asked, leaning closer. "That looks nasty."

"It feels nasty," Kerry muttered. "I was in a fight."

"You seem to be having your share of problems," Conquest said, still staring into Kerry's face. "You sure you don't want to talk to somebody? It helps, you know." He wasn't a bad guy, Kerry decided. He actually seemed like a human, something no one expects in a school administrator.

"I don't think it would help," Kerry said. "It's something I have to work out on my own."

Conquest stared at him in silence. He picked up the pipe and slapped it gently against his open palm. "Maybe we should have an assembly to talk about the vandalism that was done," he said thoughtfully.

"*No!*" Kerry jumped to his feet.

Conquest pulled back, startled, and almost toppled over backward.

"Please," Kerry said. "It would only cause more trouble. I'll take care of it. Really, I will."

"You seem to be doing a fabulous job so far," the principal said, regaining his balance and his composure. "This has to do with that accident on the football field last week, doesn't it?"

Kerry nodded.

"The Murdoch boy came out of his coma,"

Conquest said, sucking on the pipe stem.

"Oh, that's great!" Kerry cried.

"It was just shock trauma. It happens. He'll be okay now — except for the leg, of course."

"Great," Kerry repeated. It was the first good news he'd heard in a while.

"They're not allowing him to have visitors for a few days. But that's understandable. Listen, Kerry, we'll get you a new set of texts. And we won't do anything about the malicious attack on your property. . . ."

"Thanks, Mr. Conquest. I — "

"But if anything else happens, I want you to come tell me about it. Is that a deal?"

"Okay," Kerry said, getting up. What else could he say? For an instant, he thought of telling Conquest about the threatening phone calls. But he quickly decided to leave well enough alone. What could the principal do about it, anyway? Call an assembly? That would really do a whole lot of good!

He thanked Mr. Conquest again and backed out of the office. When he reached the hall, the bell for class change rang right above his head, practically startling him out of his shoes. He turned and began walking toward his first class — and bumped right into Sharon Spinner.

"Ouch!" she yelled. She was overreacting. He hadn't really bumped her that hard. "Jerk — are you gonna break *my* leg now?"

"Sharon, I want to talk to you."

"Well, that makes my heart go pitty-pat.

Did you hear that Sal is awake?"

"I just heard," Kerry said, hurrying to keep up with her as she walked as quickly as she could down the hall. "I'm so glad. Have you talked to him?"

"Not yet," she called back to him. "They won't let him take any calls or see anyone until tomorrow."

"Sharon, I've got to talk to you about the phone calls."

She didn't stop walking.

But Kerry took it as a good sign that she was talking to him at all. She still seemed angry, but her anger appeared to be in control.

"What phone calls?"

"I think you know what I'm talking about."

She spun around angrily, bumping into two other kids who happened to be walking at her side. "I don't have the time or interest for any stupid mysteries, Hart," she said, clenching her teeth and narrowing her eyes. "Who do you want to call, anyway?"

"Sharon — the calls. . . ."

The bell rang.

"Leave me alone!" she yelled, turning and running toward room 234 at the end of the nearly empty hall. "Just leave me alone! You've done enough!"

She disappeared into the classroom.

Miss MacCurdy poked her gray head out the door and stared at Kerry. "You're late, young man. Where's your class?"

He couldn't remember.

It was one more great moment to add to what was becoming a monumentally lousy day.

He thought about Mandy through all of his classes and through his two study halls. It kept his mind off everything else.

A lot of kids weren't talking to him because of what they thought he had deliberately done to Sal's leg. They made a big point of snubbing him so that he'd know their feelings.

The kids who *were* talking to him only wanted to talk about how awful he looked. This wasn't exactly a subject he wanted to pursue.

He looked for Mandy after his last class. But he couldn't find her anywhere.

He took the bus home, riding up to the hills, lost in thought, feeling sorry for himself, feeling very alone. Watching Sean lie on the couch watching reruns of old sitcoms didn't make him feel any less alone. Sean could see that Kerry was feeling pretty low. He offered to switch off the sitcoms and put on MTV — a very generous offer for Sean — but Kerry declined and went up to his room.

After a dinner of microwaved McDonald's hamburgers, Kerry went back up to his room. He decided to go to bed early. Sleep was the only escape from the aches and pains of his battered and bruised body. It was only eight o'clock, but he fell asleep quickly.

He had a vivid dream, a dream he had had before.

He saw a bright blue sky streaked with ribbons of white, puffy clouds. The sky was reflected in the smooth waters of a gently flowing river.

He and Donald were in a canoe on the river, Donald smiling lazily, rowing casually, his paddles moving slowly back and forth. Kerry, in contrast, was rowing frantically, desperately trying to keep up with Donald, even though they were in the same canoe.

Their parents — both of them — stood together on the green shore, their arms around each other, yelling encouragement to the two brothers in the canoe, waving them on.

Kerry felt wonderful. The sun beat down, making him warm and comfortable all over. The water splashed and sparkled as he and Donald moved the bright red paddles.

Donald gave him a big grin. "You're doing it, kid. You're really doing it!" he said, crinkling his eyes in that happy way. Donald was the only one in the family who could crinkle his eyes.

Faster, faster, Kerry paddled, urged on by Donald's words.

Suddenly, he had a horrible realization. He knew without seeing it that they were headed toward a sheer drop, a steep, raging waterfall.

He looked across the canoe at Donald. Donald grinned and continued paddling lazily, lying back and enjoying the hot, hot sun. Donald didn't know about the waterfall.

"You're doing wonderfully, boys," their mother, her black hair fluttering freely in the rippling river breezes, called, waving to them from shore.

Kerry realized that he was the only one who knew about the waterfall.

He knew he should tell Donald. But he kept paddling furiously.

The river flowed gently. But Kerry knew that they were only a few yards away from the drop, only a few seconds away from being hurtled over the steep waterfall.

"Great! Great, boys! I'm so proud!" their father yelled, tipping his police cap in an exaggerated salute.

Kerry kept paddling. He knew he should tell Donald — now. He struggled with himself. He wasn't going to tell. Yes — he was. No.

Why doesn't Donald know about the waterfall, too?

Why am I the only one?

Closer, closer. The blue waters began to swirl and bubble up white and frothy.

The phone woke him from the dream.

Would he have told Donald if the dream had continued? Would he have stopped paddling so furiously toward certain disaster?

He shook himself alert and stared at the clock. It was one in the morning. How long had the phone been ringing?

One o'clock in the morning.

Another call.

When would she stop? What was the point of this?

He grabbed the receiver. He was going to keep her on the line this time. He was going to get through to her. Enough was enough.

"Now listen — " he screamed into the receiver, startled by his own anger and frustration.

"Hey, man — did you meet her? What was she like?"

"Josh?"

"Yeah, it's Josh. How quickly they forget. I was only out of school for one day, Kerry."

"Sorry, I — uh — I was asleep. Dreaming, I guess."

"Since when do you have to be asleep to be dreaming?"

Kerry's heart was still racing. He took a deep breath. "Where were you today?"

"Upset stomach."

"Right. I believe it," Kerry said sarcastically.

"You'd have an upset stomach, too, if you had to look at *you!*" Josh said. "You feel any better?"

"Aces," Kerry said.

"Anyone decide to play handball with your face today?"

"No. They poured red paint in my locker instead," Kerry said.

"Cool." Josh was silent for a moment. Then he said, "At least you don't have to worry like the rest of us about being popular. You *know* everyone hates your guts!"

"Very funny," Kerry said, yawning. "Can I go back to sleep now that you've cheered me up?"

"No," Josh insisted. "What about Mandy? I didn't call to talk about you. Did you meet her? Is she as sexy in person as she is on the phone? Or is she a bow-wow with a great voice?"

"I met her," Kerry said. He had been thinking about Mandy all day and all evening. But now it was hard to think of anything to say about her. "She's real . . . nice."

"Uh-oh," Josh said. "Nice, huh."

"She's . . . sexy," Kerry admitted. "She's real different."

"Is she hot for your bod, Kerry? C'mon, man, you can tell *me*."

"Well, she's . . . uh . . . what can I say?"

"I know, I know. You're saving yourself for your wedding night. Hey — you've been real informative, Kerry. I should've dialed that city service number. At least I would've gotten the time and the temperature."

"Give me a break, Josh. I was asleep. And my head is throbbing."

"Hey, that's right," Josh said. "You must've made some impression on Mandy with a face that looks like a boiled cabbage."

"You really know how to hurt a guy," Kerry said wearily. "Hey, did you hear? Sal woke up. He came out of his coma."

"When do you come out of yours?"

"What? What did you say?"

"Hey, I'm sorry — it was a joke, Kerry. It wasn't a heavy comment or anything. That's great about Sal. Really. You're sure a little edgy tonight, aren't you?"

"Edgy? I don't know *why* I should be edgy," Kerry said. "I get beaten up. I get threatening phone calls every night. Someone fills my locker with paint. . . ."

"Don't forget that everyone in school hates your guts," Josh added.

"Right. Thanks. You're real helpful."

They both laughed.

"Okay," Josh said suddenly. "That was it. I just wanted to hear if you could still laugh. G'night." And he hung up.

Kerry sat in the dark holding the receiver tightly in his hand. "I've got weird friends," he said aloud.

He climbed back into bed, his side aching, his face throbbing. He remembered his dream. Closing his eyes, he tried to bring it back.

I wonder if Donald and I go over the rapids, he thought, frowning. He had had the dream before, several times that he remembered. Each time, he woke up in a panic, still paddling desperately just a few yards from disaster. He never saw the outcome. Maybe there wasn't one.

It took a long time to get back to sleep. He thought about Mandy. She seemed so distant in a way, even when she was holding on to him. He liked the way she touched him, the way she took his arm, even though they had just met. She seemed open, available . . . hungry. He probably could make it with her. . . .

Thinking about that excited him and kept him even farther from sleep. What was it about her that was so different from the other girls at Revere? Well, it was the blue smock, for one thing. It was so old-fashioned, so private school, so . . . out-of-it. There wasn't anything trendy about Mandy, he realized. Not her hair, not her clothes. She didn't carry her books in a backpack that had — hey, wait a minute!

She didn't carry *anything*.

He pictured her standing there by his locker when he arrived at school. Yes, she wasn't carrying anything at all — not even a pocketbook.

He wanted to think about this more, to figure out what else was different about her, but he drifted off to sleep, a heavy, dreamless sleep, all black and silent and empty.

When he came down the stairs the next morning, leaning against the banister because of the ache in his side, he was surprised to find his father waiting for him. He had his uniform on, but his tie was missing and the collar was unbuttoned and open. His eyes were red-rimmed and circled with thick, black rings. His lower lip trembled as he tried to greet Kerry.

He put his arm around Kerry's shoulder and led him toward the living room couch.

Uh-oh, Kerry thought. Something's up.

He was right.

"I got some news this morning," his father said. His throat was fogged, but he didn't bother to clear it.

"News?" Kerry asked, feeling his stomach tighten.

"Yeah. I—uh—got a call. Early. I've been waiting for you to wake up." He kept his arm around Kerry's shoulder. Kerry felt as if his father was leaning on him for support, using Kerry to stay on his feet. He had never leaned on Kerry before.

"What? What is it, Dad?"

"It's your brother Donald," Lt. Hart said. "He's escaped."

Chapter 9

Escaped?

From where?

Kerry realized — for the first time — that he didn't know where his brother was. How could that be? Had he been living in a dream-world for an entire year?

"I guess we've all been living in a dream-world," his father said, echoing Kerry's thoughts. "I've tried to protect you. The doctors said I should."

"Protect me from what?" Kerry asked. "From Donald?"

His father didn't answer. He walked to the refrigerator, pulled out a pitcher of orange juice, and poured Kerry a glass. Kerry took the glass from his father's hand and took a long, cold sip. The juice tasted bitter and pulp stuck in his throat. He took another bitter sip to wash it down. "Well, Dad — " he started, but his father had returned to the living room.

"Is Donald coming home?" Kerry asked.

Lt. Hart paced back and forth in the narrow room, rubbing his chin, lost in a turmoil of thoughts.

"Come on, Dad," Kerry demanded, trying to get through to his father. "You've got to tell me now. You really don't have a choice, do you?"

"The doctors . . . they all thought you'd remember by now," his father said, avoiding his eyes. "It would have been easier, I suppose." He turned to face his son. "Do you remember anything at all?"

Kerry closed his eyes.

"No. Not much."

"What do you mean *not much?*" Lt. Hart demanded. "Does that mean you remember *something?*"

"Headlights," Kerry said. "I see headlights. That's all, Dad. I'm sorry."

"I'm sorry, too," his father said quietly. "I'm just a cop."

"Well, then you're used to delivering bad news," Kerry said, a flash of anger revealed in his voice. Was it anger — or just impatience to know what no one would talk to him about for so many months?

"Hey, you got no cause to snap at me, fella," Lt. Hart said. "I've only tried to do what's right. It hasn't been easy. Especially with your mother gone. But I don't complain. When you're a cop, you get to see that there are two sides to life, like two sides to a coin. There's the bright side and there's the dark side."

Kerry sat down on the couch. He realized his father must really be upset. He'd never heard him launch into such philosophy before. His father babbled on about the light side and the dark side, and how one side can overwhelm the other side, and how Kerry had retreated into one side when the other side got to be too much.

Kerry didn't really hear all the words. His mind was spinning. His father's voice floated nearby, then drifted away as Kerry's own thoughts broke into his consciousness. He thought about how much he had missed Donald, how much he had relied on his older brother, how much his brother's encouragement had meant to him, and how badly he had felt when Donald had become displeased or had criticized him.

Donald had been the most important person in his life. How could he not know where Donald was? How could he not *care*?

"... at least that's what the doctors think," his father said. "But now, of course, all that is changed." He stared at Kerry from across the room. The gray morning light filtered through the window, casting more shadows than light.

"What?" Kerry struggled to hear his father. There was a fluttering in his ears, like the flapping of bird wings.

"Listen, Kerry, with Donald escaped, I got no choice. I've got to tell you a little. It isn't going to be easy for you. But — " Lt. Hart started to sit down on the couch next to Kerry, but the phone rang.

Kerry jumped up, but his father got to the phone first. "Hello?"

His eyes opened wide, then returned to narrow slits. He stood holding the receiver in silence for a few seconds, then replaced it angrily.

"Who was it?" Kerry asked.

"Some girl, probably a friend of yours," Lt. Hart said, easing himself back down onto the couch. "She started to say something. But when she realized it was me, she hung up." He groaned. His back must have been giving him pain.

Probably Sharon, calling to give him a cheerful morning death threat, Kerry thought.

"Look, Dad," Kerry said impatiently, "whatever you've got to tell me — just tell me. You're only making it worse by dragging it out like this."

"Making it worse?" Lt. Hart's face twisted into an ironic smile. "Oh boy." He seemed to drift away again. Even though he was sitting next to Kerry on the low couch, he was miles away.

The fluttering left Kerry's ears. Now, the silence seemed crushingly loud.

Say something, Dad. Say *something*!

"There was a car accident," Lt. Hart said flatly, staring at his shiny black police shoes.

"I knew it!" Kerry cried. "The headlights. . . ."

His father got up and walked over to the window. "Come on, fella. Don't interrupt. Let me just tell it. Make it a little bit easy for me, okay?"

"Sorry," Kerry said. He was as surprised by his outburst as his father. Why had he done that? He hadn't known it. He had no memory of a car accident. Why was he so quick to say that he had?

"It was a little over a year ago. In July. You were all on vacation. There was no school." His father was staring out the window as he spoke. The gray morning light washed over him, turning him gray, spreading gloom instead of warmth.

"It was late at night. There were three of you in the front seat of our car. Do you remember the car?"

Kerry thought hard. "No."

"I'm not going to give you details, Kerry. I'm only going to tell you enough — enough so you can deal with Donald's escape."

"Okay, okay," Kerry said, unable to hide his impatience, even though he could see his father was struggling with every word.

Silence.

A car rumbled by, tires spinning over pebbles in the road as it climbed the steep hill.

"It was late at night. Did I say that? Oh well, it doesn't really matter. There was an accident, a collision, down at the foot of the hills, on Edgecreek by the turn. Donald's girl friend was sitting in the middle, between you and Donald.

"It was a . . . bad crash. Her head hit the mirror. Then there was a second jolt and — "

Kerry waited. His father took a deep breath. He was a policeman, but he never got used to death.

"The girl was killed," he said quickly.

"And Donald?" Kerry asked, his voice gurgling up weakly from deep in his throat, his hands ice cold.

"Donald couldn't accept it. He cracked."

"But he was alive," Kerry demanded.

"Yeah. Untouched practically," Lt. Hart replied, seeming surprised by the question. "So were you. Just a few cuts. That scar over your eyebrow."

Kerry's hand went up to the scar. It was still a little tender. He'd never paid any attention to it except when his comb slipped or he accidentally scratched it.

"But Donald couldn't accept it that his girl friend . . . was dead. He cracked. He just snapped. We had no choice. We had to send him away — to a hospital. You know, a place for mental patients."

That's where his brother was? In a mental hospital?

"You — uh — don't remember any of this?" his father asked cautiously.

"No," Kerry muttered. "No. Headlights. Just headlights. Nothing."

"Well, I've told you most of it. Enough, I guess," Lt. Hart said, leaning on the windowsill, staring out into the gray morning. "Donald's been in the hospital ever since. I tried to see him, but the docs don't want me to. They thought he'd snap out of it better if he didn't see any of us for a while. They're probably right. I got weekly reports from them, though. I kept tabs on him. I didn't desert him up there."

"And is he better?" Kerry asked, his voice nearly a whisper.

"That's what the docs told me. They said he was gettin' better every day. Might even be home by Christmas. Then, first thing this morning, I get a call. Donald's run away. Flew the coop." He shook his head sadly.

"Maybe he just decided he had enough. Maybe he's fine now," Kerry said.

"Maybe there's a Santa Claus and he really lives at the North Pole. You know that's not the way it works," Lt. Hart said bitterly.

"Maybe he's heading home," Kerry said, ignoring his father's words, caught up in his own swirling thoughts, struggling to keep from being buried under the weight of the horrifying story he had just been told. "We'll get to see him, to talk to him. That'll be great — won't it?"

"I don't know," his father said. "I don't know." He glanced at his watch. Then he turned from the window and walked over to Kerry. "Are you okay?"

"I guess so. I still don't remember."

"It'll come back. And you'll be able to face it then. You're stronger than you think."

What an odd thing for his father to say. *You're stronger than you think.*

Kerry had never thought of himself as strong — or weak.

"I just want you to be careful," his father said, pulling on his tie and fumbling to get it into a knot. His hands were shaking too badly. He gave up after three tries and tossed the tie to the floor. "I gotta go. You know how to reach me if anything happens."

"Yeah . . . sure. Do you think Donald will be here by — "

"The hospital is two days away by car," Lt. Hart said at the door. "It's upstate, near the border. So don't plan on having lunch with your brother. I'm not too sure he'd head here anyway. He may. He may not. I thought I had to warn you. . . ."

Warn him? Did Kerry really have to be *warned* that his own brother might show up?

"Is he . . . dangerous, Dad?" Kerry could hardly get the words out.

"Get to school," his father said, trying to sound more cheerful. "We'll get through this okay. We Harts always manage to muddle through somehow."

His father couldn't bring himself to answer the question.

"Hey, where's Sean?" Kerry suddenly realized his brother was missing.

"He's at his friend Larry's. I already talked to him this morning, before you woke up," Lt. Hart said.

Lt. Hart pushed open the screen door and

stepped out onto the gravel driveway. Kerry heard the crunch of his shoes on the stones as he trudged toward his patrol car.

He ran to the door. "Hey, Dad. . . ."

Lt. Hart stopped at the door to the car and turned around. "What?"

"Dad — uh — one more question."

"Shoot." He fumbled in his pants pocket for the keys.

"The girl who died — Donald's girl friend. Was her name — "

"Amanda," his father said. He opened the door and climbed wearily into the patrol car.

Chapter 10

Kerry turned the Mustang into the parking lot and slowly cruised down the row, looking for a place to squeeze in. The lot was nearly filled even though it was only eight o'clock, and he was forced to park in the little lot near the back of the stadium.

He locked the car and walked quickly toward the gym, his sport jacket flapping in the strong October breeze, his tie squeezing his throat. Did anyone actually feel *comfortable* when they dressed up?

"What's 'a matter, Hart — couldn't get a date?" someone yelled.

He couldn't see who was calling to him, so he just kept walking. He saw Mandy waiting for him by the sidewalk at the edge of the parking lot.

"Hi!" he called, waving, but she didn't seem to see him.

He started to run, his new shoes slipping on the asphalt. She was wearing a long, purple dress, glittery, and very slinky. She held a white wrap, some kind of shawl, around her shoulders. Her blonde hair sparkled under the glow of the parking lot lamps.

She spotted him, gave him a quick wave, and started to run toward him. Her shoes clicked on the ground as she ran. Other couples heading into the gym turned to stare at her. She was a little overdressed for a simple dance in the gym.

"Mandy," he said. "Hi."

She fell into his arms.

"Sorry!" She pulled herself upright. "I tripped."

"I didn't mind," he said, trying to sound suave.

She gave him a quick kiss on the cheek. Her lips felt hot and soft. She smiled at him, bright purple lips on her pale face. They started toward the gym door. He could still feel the touch of her lips on his cheek. He wondered if she had left lipstick prints there.

"Well . . . you found the school. Amazing!" she said, taking his arm, pulling herself close to him, so close he could feel the warmth of her body.

"Was I late? I mean, am I late?" She was making him nervous. He decided he didn't mind.

"It's never too late," she whispered, putting her lips against his ear, sending chills down his body.

He opened the gym door and handed the tickets to Miss MacCurdy, who was seated at a card table just inside. "Two?" she asked. She tore the tickets in half and motioned them to go in. She didn't expect an answer.

"Golly gee, a real school dance," Mandy said sarcastically. But then her expression softened and she looked to Kerry like a little girl. "It's been so long . . ." she said softly.

The theme of the dance was fall, and the gym was decorated appropriately with large construction-paper leaves of orange and brown toppling down the walls, paper pumpkins and apples floating from the ceiling, orange and black Halloween balloons, and a mural showing a football player in a Panther uniform kicking a giant football on which appeared the words KILL 'EM, PANTHERS!

This reminder made Kerry stop short, and he quickly looked around the crowded gym to see if any of his former teammates were in attendance. He couldn't really see. The lights had been turned low. Orange and blue spotlights streaked the room with darting, dim light. The dancers and hangers-on were gray and black shadows in the swirling spotlights.

"Do you like my dress?"

He remembered Mandy, turned to look at her. She pulled back the white wrap that covered her dress, revealing how low-cut her purple gown was.

"Wow!"

'Why, Kerry, you're easily impressed," she said, laughing at his wide-eyed expression.

"No, I just — I mean — "

"I'd better put this back on," Mandy said in a teasing voice, and wrapped the white shawl tightly around herself again. "I wouldn't want you to go berserk or anything," she said, "at least not until later. . . ."

"It's a very pretty dress," Kerry managed to say. She was stacked! But somehow it was all wrong. That body on that innocent face. That dress. It didn't really seem to fit her at all. It was almost as if she was wearing someone else's dress, someone else's body.

"I'm glad you like it," she said coyly.

Someone bumped Kerry — hard — from behind.

His heart leaped. He hadn't thought. Of course the football players would be here tonight. Of course he would be easy prey for those goons — again.

He spun around, ready to fight.

"Hey, how's it goin'?"

"Josh. Hi. This is Mandy. Mandy, Josh."

"I'm Josh," Josh said, staring at Mandy's dress.

"You must be Josh," Mandy said.

"I must be, if Kerry says so," Josh said.

"Are all your friends this boring?" Mandy asked Kerry.

"No. Only Josh," Kerry said.

"Hey, thanks a lot, man," Josh said. "You want to know *boring*, Mandy — you just hang around with this guy. Ha ha!"

"I wish things *were* a little more boring,"

Kerry said suddenly, thinking he saw O'Brien and Malick walking toward him across the dance floor.

"What?" Mandy asked, surprised.

"Nothing," Kerry said. It was two other guys. Got to cool it, he told himself. They already beat the crap out of me. They're not gonna want seconds right here on the dance floor tonight.

Mandy took his hand in her cold little hand and squeezed it hard. She must have sensed that he was troubled about something. "Where's your date?" she asked Josh.

"See — over by the wall? She's the one on her knees over there," Josh said, pointing.

"I'd turn to prayer, too, if I had to go out with you," Kerry said.

"No. She lost a contact," Josh said. "Not much chance of finding it in this light, but she doesn't have a replacement. Hey — your face looks better," he added, staring at Kerry as if he were some sort of lab specimen.

"Better than what?" Mandy asked, and then laughed.

"I seem to be outnumbered here," Kerry said.

"Why don't we dance?" Mandy suggested, pulling him away. Were her hands always this freezing cold? Or was she just really nervous around Kerry?

"See you later," Josh said. "And then you're supposed to say, 'Not if I see you first.' "

She pulled Kerry into the middle of the crowded floor, squeezing between dancers moving through the flickering, dim lights, and began moving slowly to the music, still holding his hands tightly in hers, swaying softly, moving slowly even though the music was fast — some sort of salsa record with an insistent, repeating disco-type drum riff.

"Your face *is* better," she called to him over the music.

"It's the dark lights," he said, trying to follow her but finding it difficult since she wasn't keeping to the music.

"You have a nice face," she said.

Someone bumped the tone arm of the record player. It scratched through the salsa record. There was a short, silent pause. Then a ballad with slow, sexy rhythms started up.

She began to push Kerry back as they danced, back toward the wall containing the football player mural. Her eyes were closed, her dark lips spread in a wide smile, her face tilted up at his. Back, she guided him, back. They began to dance well together, began to move together, back, back to the wall. . . .

When they reached the wall, twisting shadows of dancing couples darting and flickering on the crudely painted mural, she pushed him gently until his back was against the mural. Then she put her hands on the back of his neck, pulled his head down, and raised her purple lips up to meet his.

He was so surprised, he gasped. Her lips were hot and soft and she pushed them against his, harder and harder. At first, he tried to return the kiss. But as she pressed harder, her teeth hungrily pushing against his lips, he tried to back away, to end the kiss, to catch his breath.

But she held him in a firm grip, her cold hands tight on the back of his neck. Her kiss, as she pushed against him, became painful. It wasn't a kiss. It was an attack. Her teeth dug harder against him. Her tongue pushed against his. . . .

Finally, she sighed and retreated.

He took a deep breath. Before he could say anything, she pulled his head down to her mouth again. She whispered into his ear, her breath hot, her lips brushing his ear as she spoke. "Sorry, Kerry. Sometimes I'm a little . . . impulsive."

She backed away and let go of his head. Her mouth formed a shy smile. She looked embarrassed. She whispered, "It was nice," turned, and ran onto the dance floor, disappearing in the swaying shadows of dancers.

Kerry started after her, but stopped. He leaned back against the wall. He put a hand up to his throbbing lips. His lips were bleeding.

He looked for her, bumping into dancers who gave him annoyed looks, tripping over feet, searching the shadows formed by the revolving lights. Had she left the gym? Was she coming back?

"Hey, man — she's a fox!" Josh called to him.

Jessie, his date, hadn't found her contact. She was dancing with one eye squinted. She squinted at Kerry in greeting.

"You noticed," Kerry called, trying to sound nonchalant, hoping that Josh wouldn't ask where Mandy was.

"Where's Mandy, anyway?" Josh called. He was a terrible dancer. He looked like a duck when he danced, wobbling from side to side.

"Girls' room," Kerry answered, searching the crowd.

"Later," Josh said. He waddled off, Jessie squinting after him.

Kerry made his way to the gym door. Miss MacCurdy was still sitting at the admissions table, guarding the door. She frowned when she saw Kerry approaching. She doesn't like me, he thought. Then he thought, She doesn't really like anybody.

"Did my date go out this way?" he asked her.

She frowned again. "The one in the purple dress?"

"Yeah."

"No. I haven't seen her. Maybe we should set up a booth for lost dates. Ha ha ha!"

"Thanks." She was still laughing as Kerry disappeared back into the crowd. His lips still throbbed. He could still feel the hot touch of her lips against his ear as she whispered, her cold little hands on the back of his neck.

Sometimes I'm a little . . . impulsive.

He wanted to go off in a corner and think about her. Why did she kiss him like that? Was it just a sudden impulse? Did she really like him? Or was she playing some sort of game with him?

She was so quick-witted, so sophisticated, so together. But she was terribly overdressed, embarrassingly overdressed, and she didn't seem to be at all aware of it. And she was always clinging to him, always pulling him, always touching him. Was that because she was nervous — or was she trying to make *him* nervous?

It occurred to Kerry that maybe she was *trying* to be mysterious. If so, he thought, she was sure succeeding!

He walked past the long refreshment table, with its big glass jugs of apple cider, pumpkin breads, raisin cookies, and other not terribly tempting items, most of which had been baked in home ec. classes. No sign of her. Was she playing hide and seek with him? Was she embarrassed about the impulsive kiss?

Then his eye caught someone slipping out of the gym through the door that led into the classroom corridor. Was that Mandy? He quickly made his way back through the crowded dance floor. He pushed open the double doors and stepped into the dark corridor.

He heard footsteps not far away. "Mandy?"

No reply.

He looked down the dark row of lockers. Only a small light at the far end of the corridor had been turned on. They obviously didn't want kids leaving the gym and wandering around in the school.

He heard footsteps in the direction of the light.

"Mandy — is that you?" he tried again.

Still no reply.

He began walking quickly toward the light. The empty corridor seemed eerie, even though it was so familiar. Without lights, without kids clattering their lockers, talking and shouting, it seemed like a tunnel, a tunnel of weird shadows and misplaced echoes.

His footsteps sounded thunderous, clicking against the floor, echoing off the metal lockers. "Mandy?" His voice was a loud whisper. At the light, he stopped. He heard voices to the right. It was too dark to see who it was, so he started toward the voices. "Mandy?"

"Hey — Hart!"

Two figures emerged in the dark corridor.

Malick and O'Brien.

"Hey — Hart! Wait up!" They began running toward him.

He turned and ran the other way. If only he had stayed in the gym! They wouldn't have tried any rough stuff surrounded by hundreds of dancers and the teachers. But now he was easy prey, alone in the dark, empty hallway, no one around.

"Hart! Stop!"

He ran as fast as he could. But they were narrowing the gap.

Weren't these guys ever apart? he thought. Had they come to the dance together? Despite his fear, he smiled as he ran. He pictured them dancing together, a slow dance, cheek to cheek.

"Give up, Hart!"

If he kept running straight, they'd catch up to him in a few seconds. He saw the double cafeteria doors up ahead to the left. If he could get into the dark cafeteria, he could hide under a table or in the kitchen. He'd stand a tiny chance of getting away from them.

His heart pounding, he stopped at the double doors, turned quickly to see that his pursuers were less than a hundred yards behind him, and heaved his shoulder into the cafeteria doors.

They were locked.

"No!" he cried aloud.

"Hart! Hart — you moron!"

He lunged for the stairway across from the cafeteria, practically flung himself down the tile steps, stumbling, his new shoes slipping, groping down the rail. He landed hard on his feet in the basement, which was darker than the other hallway. Gasping for breath, he ran.

The maintenance room was straight ahead. He could duck inside. There'd be plenty of places to hide — if the door wasn't locked.

He heard their footsteps on the stairs. They were right behind him.

A dim light shone through the small, round window in the door to the maintenance room. He pushed at the door.

Locked.

He could feel the dread tightening his stomach, tightening his neck muscles. He pressed himself flat against the narrow recess in front of the door. Maybe Malick and O'Brien would run right past him and he could get back upstairs to the safety of the crowded gym. He tried to hold his breath. He tried to think invisible thoughts.

"Hart — you chicken! Hey, Malick — here he is!" O'Brien called.

"Now, wait a minute — " Kerry started, raising his fists.

"Malick — over here!" O'Brien called, looming over Kerry in the dark.

Malick came lumbering over. They stood side by side, smiling at Kerry as they closed in on him. . . .

Chapter 11

O'Brien pressed a big fist against Kerry's chest, pinning him to the door. Kerry looked into their smiling faces, reflected in the dim light.

This can't be happening to me, he told himself. I'm not going to get creamed again by these goons.

"Hey, Hart — cool it," O'Brien said, shaking his head.

"Yeah, cool it," Malick repeated.

"We owe you an apology," O'Brien said.

"What?" Kerry's voice was a squeak.

"You heard me," O'Brien said, loosening his grip on Kerry's chest, his beefy face floating ominously in the dim yellow light.

"It was all a misunderstanding," Malick said. "We saw Sal today. At the hospital. He set us straight."

Kerry was still breathing too hard to talk. What were they saying? The words weren't making sense to him. "How's Sal?" he finally managed to say.

"He's doin' better," O'Brien said. "It ain't been a picnic, but he'll be okay."

"Good," Kerry uttered, trying to stop the two faces from floating in front of him. "That's good."

"Sal said the whole thing was an accident," Malick said. "He said you fell on him 'cause you couldn't stop."

"He don't blame you," O'Brien added. "He saw the whole thing. He saw you didn't do it on purpose."

"Of course not," Kerry said, brightening.

But then he had a shudder of horror. Was this another one of his daydreams? Was he imagining this whole scene? Would he blink, open his eyes in a second, and find them ready to pound the life out of him again, leaving him a pile of pulp for the janitor to clean up on Monday morning?

Kerry blinked. He opened his eyes.

"Anyway," Malick said, "no hard feelings." He stuck out a meaty hand for Kerry to shake.

Kerry shook his hand. Then he shook O'Brien's hand. "No hard feelings," O'Brien said.

"Hey, you're still a little puke," Malick said, tapping Kerry hard on the knot of his tie. "But we wanted to set the record straight."

They turned and walked off into the darkness. Kerry waited, listened to them climb the stairs. "What a dork," he heard O'Brien say. He heard them both laugh. Their laughter and the footsteps grew fainter, then faded to silence.

Kerry stood in the dark doorway for a few more minutes, getting himself together. He began to feel pretty good. He realized that word would get around about what Sal had said, about how it was all an accident. Maybe people would start talking to him again, start treating him as if he didn't have bubonic plague. And the pranks would stop. And no more late-night threatening phone calls.

"Okay!" he called out to no one.

He walked to the stairway and began climbing the stairs two at a time. He could hear the music from the gym, pounding drums, loud saxophones. Mandy. . . .

He had almost forgotten about her.

He had to find her. He wanted to tell her what had happened, how good he felt.

He wanted to dance; he wanted to shout!

Maybe they could leave the dance and go be impulsive somewhere together!

He pushed open the door to the gym and was assaulted by a wave of heat and noise, by twirling purple lights, weaving and swaying dancers, a roar of talk and laughter.

"Hey — Mandy!"

There she was, standing by herself at the end of the refreshment table, a cup of cider in her hand.

"Mandy — where'd you go?"

"Never mind that. Where'd *you* go? I've been looking all over for you." She took his arm. Her hands felt warm for the first time. "Want some cider? It's pretty good, if you like cider. I thought maybe you had run away. You wouldn't run away, would you, Kerry? You like me, don't you?"

She was talking a mile a minute. Why was *she* so worked up? He was the one who was excited.

"Two of the Panthers just apologized to me," he told her, putting his arm around her waist.

She pulled away, out of his grasp. "What?"

"Sal told them it was all a mistake. So they apologized. I'm not the school villain anymore."

"That's nice," she said, looking at him as if he were speaking another language. "I never thought you were a villain," she said, returning to her kittenish voice and resting her head on his shoulder for just a second.

He was suddenly very thirsty. He poured a cup of cider, then another. It was sweet and cold. He smiled at Mandy, who returned his smile with a devilish one of her own, a wisp of blonde hair floating gently down her pale forehead.

"Let's dance," she said, pulling him with both hands. "I don't want you to run away again. Do you hear?"

Kerry smiled and followed her onto the crowded floor. It seemed to him that she had it all backward. It was *she* who had run away. But he didn't feel like arguing with her. The music was soft and slow, an old

Carpenters' record they always played at dances, "We've Only Just Begun," and she felt warm and small pressed against him . . . warm, small, and exciting.

They danced a lot without talking much. The evening passed quickly. They were playing "The Last Dance," a Donna Summer record, and then the bright gym lights were turned on — and the dance was over.

Mandy put her arm around his waist as they made their way through the exit to the parking lot. Josh gave Kerry a thumbs-up sign from across the gym. Kerry wanted to talk to Josh, to tell him about his apologies from O'Brien and Malick. Josh would be as surprised as Kerry. But he couldn't get over to Josh, and he lost him in the crowd of kids pushing their way through the single, narrow exit.

The cold air hit their faces as they stepped outside. It was cold enough for a frost. Kerry hoped the Mustang would start. It was even more finicky in cold weather.

Mandy grinned up at him.

"What's so funny?" he asked, pulling her close.

"Nothing. Just thinking," she said coyly.

"Thinking? That can be dangerous," he said.

"Where's the car?" she asked.

"Oh, I had to park it in front of my house. I couldn't find a place down here. It's a short walk — five or six miles uphill. You don't mind, do you?"

She laughed and shook her head. "You're funny," she said quietly, and gave his hand a hard squeeze.

"I'm sorry you didn't get to talk to Josh more," he said. "He's very funny. He's the funniest guy I know."

"How long have you been friends?" she asked, her breath smoking in the cold air. She pulled the white shawl around her shoulders. It really wasn't warm enough for the cold night.

I'll find a way to keep her warm, Kerry thought.

It's funny, he thought. He was walking along with her, talking about Josh, but he was thinking about sex. He decided that wasn't strange at all. That's what he always did when he was with a girl. He talked about some subject or another and thought about sex. He wondered if Mandy was doing the same thing. He hoped she was.

"We've walked six miles. Where's the car?" she asked.

"It's right here," he said. He stopped.

His mouth dropped open.

"Oh no!"

He shook his head.

No. No. No. This can't be happening.

The tires on the Mustang were slashed to ribbons. All four of them. Pieces of rubber lay strewn across the aisle of the parking lot. Someone had slashed the tires, and slashed and slashed at them until pieces had been torn clear off.

Mandy stared at the car, which looked so weird resting at such a low angle. Then she screamed and buried her head in Kerry's shoulder.

"Oh my god, Kerry," she said, her voice shaking. "This is getting scary!"

Chapter 12

"I — I can't bear to look at it," Mandy cried, burying her head in Kerry's shoulder. "It's so . . . vicious."

Kerry was so upset and surprised by the sight of the shredded rubber, he hadn't noticed that the windshield and front side windows had been shattered. A giant, spreading spider web of cracks covered the windshield, illuminated by the stadium light. Triangles and squares of broken glass lay strewn on both sides of the car.

Vicious was the right word.

The word sent a sudden chill down his body. He shuddered. He looked around the darkening parking lot. The last cars were pulling away. Was the person who had done this to his car waiting around somewhere nearby, watching gleefully, feeling happy and satisfied, gloating over another successful attack on the well-being of Kerry Hart?

"Someone must hate you *so much* . . ." Mandy said.

She was so frightened by the sight of the battered car, she didn't realize that her words were scaring him even more.

"I'll get you home and then deal with the car," he said, his arm around her. He was shivering even though she was pressed against him. He made a conscious effort to stop shaking, then gave up when he saw that he couldn't stop, that his shivers were caused by fear, not cold.

He heard a scrabbling sound in the bushes at the side of the stadium wall. He peered into the darkness toward the sound. Was someone there? Was someone waiting for him, watching his every move?

As he stared, shivering, at the unmoving bushes, someone grabbed him from behind.

He spun around. His throat had tightened. He couldn't breathe.

"Josh!" he managed to get out.

"Didn't scare you, did I?" Josh said. Jessie, his date, still squinting, giggled.

Then they saw the Mustang.

"Oooh, man," Josh said. "Bad parking job."

"It isn't funny," Mandy said sharply.

"She's right, Josh," Jessie said quickly. "Kerry — this is awful."

Josh got very quiet. He was thinking hard.

Kerry realized that Josh knew all about the car accident the year before. Maybe he was thinking about that, seeing Kerry's car all smashed like this. Of course, he wouldn't mention it if he *was* thinking about it.

"Do you think O'Brien and Malick did this?" Josh asked. "Those jerks would do anything if they thought — "

"No," Kerry said quietly, trying not to let them see how badly he was shivering. "They didn't do it. They apologized to me about last Sunday. Sal told them what happened to him was an accident."

"They *apologized*? This is a weird evening."

"Why don't we give you both a lift home?" Jessie suggested.

"Yeah," Kerry agreed quickly. He had to sit down. He had to get out of that dark lot, away from the mutilated car. "Good idea."

"Good idea," Josh repeated, his mind elsewhere.

"No!" Mandy said suddenly. "No!" she repeated, so loudly that it startled everyone. "That's okay. Really. There's the bus. I'll just take the bus." She began running toward the bus stop, waving to the driver to stop.

"Hey, Mandy — " Kerry called after her.

"I'll call you. 'Night!" she called back. She was running at top speed across the parking lot to the bus.

"No — wait!" Kerry started running after her. But she jumped into the bus and it pulled away. He watched her standing in the aisle even though she was the only passenger. He stood watching until the bus became two red taillights against the darkness, and then faded completely from view.

"That's strange," he said with a shrug,

walking quickly back to Josh and Jessie.

"Was it something I said?" Josh asked.

Jessie gave him a poke in the ribs. "Stop it, Josh."

"She was very upset about . . . this," Kerry said, gesturing to his pitiful-looking wreck of a car. "I guess she just wanted to get away from it."

"Right," Josh agreed, a little too quickly.

Why *had* Mandy run off like that? Kerry wondered. She really had seemed more frightened and upset than *he* was. So why didn't she want a ride home in the safety of Josh's car, among friends?

The three of them crossed the empty parking lot to Josh's car, his father's new Oldsmobile Cutlass. "Who would want to do a thing like that to you, Kerry?" Jessie asked, her hands pushed tightly into the pockets of her large down coat.

"Only about three hundred kids that I can think of," Josh said, refusing to be grim despite Jessie's pokes and dirty looks.

"But Sal explained to O'Brien and Malick that — " Kerry began, his voice coming out a whine, his body shivering nonstop now.

"He didn't explain to everyone in school!" Josh said, starting up the car.

"This wasn't a typical prank," Jessie said, her analytical mind working hard. Jessie was a science freak, and she approached every problem, everything that happened in her life, with the thoroughness of a scientist.

"This seems to be the work of a *crazy* person!"

"Jessie — stop!" Josh said heatedly.

A crazy person?

A *crazy* person? The words repeated in Kerry's mind. Crazy?

Donald.

Donald was crazy.

At least he was in a place for crazy people.

Only, he had escaped.

Would his own brother be out there now, plotting against him, lying in wait for him, attacking his car — ready to attack him?

No. Not Donald.

Why would he even think such a thing?

"I'm really losing it," Kerry said aloud.

"Stay cool," Josh said. "I'll take you home so you can call your dad. At least, when *you* call the police, you know they'll come running!"

"I don't get that," Jessie said. She had just started at Revere. She didn't know Kerry's dad was a cop.

As Josh explained it to her, Kerry kept thinking about Donald. He had asked his father if he had any reason to be afraid of Donald. His father hadn't answered him.

If only he could remember what had happened . . . the accident . . . the girl. . . .

But he couldn't.

He could conjure up a flash of headlights, a screech of brakes, a scream, a cry of pain. . . .

That was a little more than before. But that was all.

And now a year later, he was riding through the darkness, shivering uncontrollably, wondering if Donald, his best friend, his . . . *idol* . . . had reason to come after him, to attack.

It was too insane.

"Here we are," Josh said, stirring Kerry from his troubled thoughts. "Hey — you're home."

Kerry shook his head. "Sorry."

"Want us to come in with you?" Jessie asked.

"No," Kerry answered quickly. "No, I'll be fine. Really." Would he be fine? Was someone waiting here in the bushes, waiting by the side of the house, waiting to grab him when he stepped out of the car?

Stop it! he told himself. Just stop it. Right *now*!

"Thanks for the lift," he said, trying to disguise the quivering of his voice, the shaking of his entire body. He knew he'd be okay once he got inside. "I'll be fine. I'll call you tomorrow, Josh."

"Yeah," Josh said, yawning. "If there's anything I can do to help. . . ."

"Thanks," Kerry said, climbing out of the car. He wanted to run inside the house as fast as he could. But he walked deliberately, slowly, up to the front stoop, turned and waved to them as they backed down into the sloping street, and then unlocked the door with a shaking hand, and pulled himself quickly inside.

He threw his coat on the floor and walked straight to the bathroom, where he was sick for a long time, violently, painfully sick. When he was finished, the trembling seemed to have stopped. He washed his face for a long time.

He felt a little better. Tired but better.

He walked quickly into the kitchen and turned on the light. Sean had been there and left. There were torn slices of bologna and Swiss cheese on the table, a used plate with bread crusts, spilled potato chips, and a half-empty glass of Coke.

He frowned at Sean's sloppiness. He felt suddenly light-headed. He guessed it was from vomiting so hard. He sat down on a kitchen chair until the dizziness passed. His mouth tasted sour. He thought he might be sick again.

He picked up the kitchen phone receiver. He hoped his dad could come home right away. He'd be angry and upset about the car, but Kerry would be real glad to see him anyway.

There was no dial tone.

Just silence.

Had someone cut the line?

Stop it, Kerry, he told himself. Stop this paranoid craziness. You've *got* to!

Still silence. No dial tone.

"Hello," he said to the silence.

"Hello — Kerry?" a voice answered back. Someone was on the line.

"Yes?"

"Kerry — I'm going to break every bone in your body. Every bone will crack, every bone will bend and break." The voice was harsh, filled with venom.

"Sharon, don't you know that — "

But he suddenly knew it wasn't Sharon. He realized it wasn't her voice. It couldn't be her voice.

"You will die, Kerry," the voice continued, machinelike, all hatred and menace. "But first you will suffer. Soon. I promise. First the bones will break — smash, smash, just like your car — then you will die."

She hung up.

She knew about the car. Whoever it was knew about the slashed tires and battered windows. And it wasn't Sharon. He knew now that it wasn't. He could hear that it wasn't.

The voice was familiar, though. He realized that it was a voice he had known. Was it a voice from his childhood? A voice from his recent past, from the year he couldn't remember?

The shakes had started again. He knew he was going to be violently ill again, too.

He dialed the police station, the special number that only families could use. A few seconds later, his dad was on the line. "Dad, it's Kerry. I think you'd better come home. . . ."

His father seemed about to explode when Kerry told him about the car. But seeing Kerry pale and shaking, he stifled the outburst before it began, and immediately assumed a professional attitude. "There probably aren't any prints worth dusting for, but I'll have Wainright give it a try in the morning," he said in his Renko drawl.

Kerry was relieved that his father had decided to play the role of policeman rather than outraged parent. He was often surprised by how considerate his father, normally a gruff and self-interested person, could be toward him. But then it suddenly dawned on Kerry that his father had been considerate of his feelings for an entire year, careful of every word he said, always on his guard not to start anything or say anything that would disturb his son or his son's memory. No wonder his father looked so much older. No wonder he had spent so little time at home. Being with Kerry was a constant strain.

"It could have been someone on the football team," Kerry said, fighting the shakes.

"Hmmm," his father said, eyeing him thoughtfully. "Let's talk about it in the morning. I think you've had enough for one night. We'll get the car towed over to O'Malley's for an estimate. And then we can talk. Okay?"

Kerry smiled. "Sure." He started toward the stairway to his room. The phone rang.

He and his father stared at each other.

The phone rang again.

"Dad, could you answer it? I've been getting some weird calls."

"I'm not surprised, with your friends. What other kind of calls could you get?" It was a feeble attempt at humor, but Kerry appreciated it.

His father picked up the kitchen phone. "Hello?" he said, sounding annoyed. "Yeah. Yeah, he's here. Are you one of his weird callers?"

Kerry cringed. Maybe having his dad answer was a bad idea.

His father handed him the phone. "Someone named Mandy," he said. "Said she was your date tonight. She doesn't sound too weird to me."

"I'll take it upstairs. 'Night, Dad. Thanks." His legs felt weak as he climbed the stairs. He picked up the phone and carried it over to the bed. "Hello?" He couldn't keep the weariness from his voice.

"I'm insulted," Mandy said, sounding kittenish.

"Why?"

"Your father said I wasn't weird."

"That's only because he hasn't met you," Kerry said. They both laughed.

"I'm sorry I ran off like that. *That* must've seemed pretty weird," Mandy said. "But I just had to get away. It was so . . . ugly."

"Yeah," Kerry said.

"I had a nice time. I mean . . . I had fun with you."

"Me, too," he said. He wanted to get under the covers.

"Was your dad mad about the car?"

"Of course. But he's a cop. So he skipped being mad and went right into the plans for the investigation," Kerry said.

"Want to get together tomorrow?" she asked. "I didn't get to give you your good-night kiss." She giggled. Was she teasing him?

If it was going to be anything like the painful kiss she'd given him in the gym, he'd just as soon skip it, Kerry decided. His hand went up to his lip, which was still swollen and painful. "Tomorrow is Monday."

"But there's no school," she said quickly. "Teachers' meetings. Come on. Meet me in the afternoon. Meet me at that coffee shop a few blocks from the school. You know, with the striped awning and the big ice-cream cone in the window."

"Phil's?"

"Yeah. Phil's. Meet me there at three. I'd really like to talk to you."

"Okay. Good," he said. What a switch! A girl was pleading with him to meet her.

"Good-night, Kerry," she whispered. Wow! She was sexy! "You know, I think pretty soon, you and I are going to have something really special going." And she hung up before he could say a word.

* * *

"I hear you got the car creamed." That was Sean's greeting at breakfast the next morning.

"Shut up, Sean," their father said, standing over a skillet of scrambled eggs.

"You're up early," Kerry said to his brother, who was seated at the kitchen table in pajama top and underpants.

"It was a mistake," Sean muttered. "I forgot there was no school."

"He'll probably go right back to bed after breakfast," Lt. Hart said, stirring the eggs vigorously, so vigorously a large chunk of them fell out of the pan and onto the stove.

"How'd you know?" Sean said.

Breakfast was spent avoiding the topic of what had happened. After breakfast, Lt. Hart handed Kerry a large manila envelope. "Insurance forms," he said. "I want you to deliver them for me to the insurance office. Do it this morning, okay? It's over on Grand Street. You know — in the civic center."

"You don't want me to come with you to look at the car?"

"No. I think I know how to look at a car. Take the forms. I'll call you later to see how you're doin'." He looked deeply into Kerry's eyes as if looking for answers to all kinds of deep problems, then quickly looked away.

Kerry started toward the stairs. "Hey, Dad — "

"Yeah?"

"You don't think that . . . Donald . . . uh. . . ."

"Donald? Wreck the car?" Lt. Hart looked more troubled than surprised by the suggestion. "Kerry, what makes you say that?"

"I don't know."

"Oh. I thought —" He caught himself. After all this time, Kerry was realizing how careful his father always was around him. *As if Kerry was a mental patient, too.*

For some reason, that thought stayed with him as he dressed, left the house, and caught the bus that would take him across town to the civic center.

The thought was still circling his head — along with thoughts of Mandy, nice thoughts about Mandy — after he had dropped off the envelope for his father. He was walking up Grand Street, his hands in his pockets, not really noticing what was in the store windows — and he bumped into someone.

"Ow! Hey — Kerry! It's you! Why don't you watch where you're going?"

"Margo! I don't believe it! I mean — I'm sorry."

Margo Fremont smiled at him. She looked the same except her hair was shorter. Her smile quickly faded. "You look awful!"

"An accident," he said.

His choice of words seemed to startle her. She jumped a little. Of course, she knew all about his accident the year before, too. Everyone knew. Everyone knew but Kerry.

"I got into a little fight."

"That's not like you," she said, grinning. "How are things at Revere? Do they miss me?"

"That's all anyone talks about," Kerry said. "When will Margo come back and pay us a visit? The place isn't the same. It's fallen apart. The walls are crumbling, everything, since you left."

"I'm at Worthinghill now," she said, rolling her eyes. "I'm learning how to be snooty. Snooty 101. That's my first course. You learn to talk through your teeth without moving your jaw."

"You always were kinda preppy, Margo. Admit it."

She put her nose in the air. "Preppy? We don't associate with preppies. They're so *common*, don't you know."

"Listen," he said, suddenly remembering that he wanted to thank her. "Mandy is terrific."

"What?"

"Mandy — she's really great," he said.

"I'm glad to hear it," Margo said. For some reason, she was being sarcastic. "Who the hell is Mandy?"

"Come on, Margo — you know. The girl you fixed me up with. The blind date. That was really nice of you. I tried to call you, but you weren't home."

"Mandy? Mandy who?"

"You're putting me on — right?"

"Kerry, somebody's putting you on. But, honey, it ain't me!"

"You don't know Mandy Lawrence?"

"Huh-uh." She shook her head to be more emphatic.

"You didn't fix me up with a blind date?"

"Kerry, if your voice gets any higher, I'll have to rent a hot air balloon and fly up to hear you. No, I'm not. No, I don't. And no, I didn't."

Kerry was absolutely speechless.

"Glad to hear she's great," Margo said sarcastically. "Did she really call you up and say that I told her to?"

"I think so . . ." Kerry said, his mind trying to recapture that first conversation. "I was sure she said that you — "

"Well . . . maybe she thought she knew me or something. I don't know. Maybe you mixed me up with somebody else, although I really don't see how it would be possible."

Kerry didn't hear a word she was saying. There was something very strange about this. Mandy had definitely said it was Margo. More than once.

"Uh . . . great seeing you, Margo. Bye." He walked down the street, his mind spinning.

"Yeah. Sure. Great seeing you, too!" Margo called after him. She shook her head and headed off in the other direction.

Kerry was glad he was meeting Mandy in a few hours. He had to confront her with this. He had to find out the truth.

For too long, he decided, the truth was something he had shut away in a forgotten corner of his brain. He made up his mind he was not going to do that anymore. He was going to confront the truth — no matter how much pain it caused, no matter what the danger was.

He waited for an hour and a half at Phil's, but Mandy didn't show up.

Chapter 13

The phone was ringing when he got home.

"Hi, Kerry. I'm sorry. I got hung up."

"Mandy — I tried to call you. But Information had no listing. They didn't have any listing at all for Lawrence."

There was a short silence. "That's because the phone must be in my mom's name," she said unconvincingly. Or was Kerry just becoming suspicious of everyone and everything? "Frances. That's her name. She doesn't always use my dad's name."

"Oh. I see. Where were you? I wanted to talk to you."

"I wanted to talk to you, too." All of the soft sexiness was gone from her voice now. She sounded anxious, worried. "I really wanted to — uh — listen, how about tonight?"

"I don't know. I don't have a car. Dad doesn't like me to — "

"I can get a car," she said quickly. "I'll pick you up at seven-thirty, okay? We'll just drive around. We'll cruise Main Street. You know — like in the movies."

He laughed. "You just want to park," he said. "I know your kind."

"I might," she said, her teasing voice back.

"You might be talking me into this," he said, cheering up. So *what* if Margo hadn't fixed them up? he thought to himself. She was still terrific. She was about the only thing that was going right for him.

"So I'll pick you up at seven-thirty?"

"You've got a date," he said. When he hung up the phone, he had a broad smile on his face.

"I don't know what you're smiling about," Lt. Hart said, walking into the kitchen, grabbing a handful of cookies from an open bag, and stuffing them into his mouth two at a time. "The mmmph mmmph mmmmph mmmpph."

"What?" Kerry asked.

His father swallowed. "The car is going to cost more than six hundred dollars."

"Have some more cookies," Kerry said.

They sat down at the kitchen table and had a long talk. Kerry told him just about everything that had happened to him since the accident on the practice field that had broken Sal's leg. He started slowly, reluctantly, not sure how much he wanted to reveal, how much of the pain, how much of the fear he wanted to share with his father. But then it all came out in a torrent of words: the threats, the phone calls late at night, the practical jokes, the friends who no longer talked to him, the beating on the basketball court — everything.

His father rubbed the bridge of his nose with his fingers, closed his eyes, tilted back the kitchen chair. Every once in a while he'd make a note, jotting a few words in a fast scribble on a small white pad. A few times, he shook his head wearily, as if to say, "These kids today. . . ."

Kerry told him everything that had happened except for his growing relationship with Mandy. Somehow he felt that to include that with all of the horrors of the past few weeks would be to taint it, to ruin it in some way. He needed to keep the one good thing happening to him private. He had to keep it separate, and clean.

"Who is this girl who called last night, this Mandy?" his father asked. Lt. Hart was not a bad policeman. He never let a detail slip by him.

Kerry smiled, impressed. "She was a blind date. She lives on Sizemore. Her family just moved here. She just started at Revere. We — she's okay. I mean, I kinda like her."

"You gonna see her again?" His father jotted something down.

"Yeah. Tonight."

Lt. Hart frowned. "You probably shouldn't go out much at night for a while, not until we figure out who's been doing all this."

The threat of not being able to see Mandy made Kerry angry. "Well, Dad, I can't just pull a shell over my head like a turtle."

"I didn't mean that. I just think that — "

"Well, we're only going to drive around. We're not going anywhere," Kerry said, sounding childish and knowing it.

"Only going to drive around, huh?" His father laughed. He pulled himself up to his feet. "Well, I don't know. You can get into an awful lot of trouble without getting out of the car, y'know, fella?" He laughed again.

Kerry could feel his face turning red. He never liked it when his dad teased him about sex.

"I gotta go in to the station," Lt. Hart said, looking for his cap. "We've got a real problem here, Kerry. This has all gone beyond the teenage-prank stage. I don't know how seriously we should take the death threats from this girl on the phone — probably not serious at all. But you never know. It wouldn't hurt to play it safe, lie low for a while till we flush this person or persons out." He found the cap on the mantel and pulled it down onto his bald head. "I know you're not going to like this. But I've gotta get the school involved in the investigation."

"Dad — " Kerry stopped before he began. He knew there was no way he could stop his father. And his father was right. He'd had enough of the threats and the fear. He was happy that his dad was getting involved in this. He nodded and didn't say anything.

Lt. Hart put a hand on Kerry's shoulder,

then headed toward the door and his patrol car. "Be careful, son."

"Yeah. Sure, Dad. Thanks."

"Call me for any reason, okay?"

"Yeah. Okay."

The door slammed. Kerry sat at the kitchen table, staring at the chair that had just held his father. He felt a little better. Somehow it made him feel more secure just having told the details to his father.

He felt secure for nearly a minute.

Then the phone rang.

The fear jumped back into his chest.

He let it ring. Again. Again.

He began to shake.

This was crazy!

He had to answer it. He couldn't live in terror of the telephone.

He picked up the receiver and lifted it slowly to his ear. "Hello?"

There was loud static at the other end, the sound you hear from pay phones on crowded street corners.

"Hello?" Kerry repeated.

"Kerry — "

He recognized the voice immediately, even though he hadn't heard it in over a year.

"Kerry, this is Donald."

"Donald?" Kerry's voice came out weak and small. His hand was trembling so hard he could barely hold the receiver.

"Kerry — be careful. I'm coming."

Slam.

What happened?

Oh no! Kerry thought.

He had accidentally hung up. Without thinking, he had slammed down the receiver.

His heart pounding in his chest, he sat and stared at the phone, waiting for Donald to call back.

But he didn't.

Those words — Donald's words — were they meant to be reassuring?

"Be careful. I'm coming."

Why did they sound like a threat?

Chapter 14

It got dark so early in the fall. By five-thirty the sun was down behind the hills. By seven-thirty it was as black as midnight, and the air was cold and heavy with frost.

Kerry stood at the living room window, staring into the blackness, waiting for Mandy, thinking about Donald. A straight black cloud, narrow as a ribbon, floated across the moon, cutting it into two half moons. Normally, he wouldn't have even noticed it. But tonight he was looking for signs, signs of strangeness, omens of what was to happen. He felt uncomfortable, out of place in his own body.

He wasn't an emotional person. Ask anyone. They'd describe him as easy going, maybe even bland. Donald had always been the one for tantrums and emotional scenes, long, heated arguments that ended in screaming and tears. Not Kerry. He'd walk away from any kind of dispute, or make a joke.

But tonight he felt . . . different. He kept

having the urge to cry. Then it would disappear and he'd feel really happy, too happy. He was on an emotional roller coaster, and as seven-thirty drew near, the ride went faster, the emotions changed more rapidly.

Guess I'm just tired, he told himself.

At a quarter to eight Mandy pulled up the hill and honked her horn. He stared out the window at the car she was driving. It was a brand new Pontiac Firebird. The two halves of the divided moon reflected off the shiny hood.

He jogged out of the house, letting the screen door slam behind him. She pushed open the car door and the light came on inside. He saw that the car was black with bright red interior, shiny red leather bucket seats, and a red dashboard. "Well, I'm impressed," he said, leaning into the car and rubbing his hand over the leather seat back.

"It doesn't take much to impress you, does it?" she said, grabbing his arm and pulling him down onto the low bucket seat. She squeezed his hand and held onto it. "I hope you don't spend the whole night talking about the car. You haven't even looked at me. I'm jealous already."

He looked at her. She was wearing jeans and a big wool poncho, a furry, loose-fitting poncho with sixties-style fringe all down the front. "I like your — uh — sweater thing," he said, pulling on a strand of fringe.

"Really? I made it." She smiled, pleased at the compliment.

"It must have taken a long time," he said.

"I *had* a long time," she said, her smile fading.

"So where'd you get this *boss* car?"

She leaned forward, put the car into drive, and began to turn it around. "Listen, I'm really sorry about this afternoon. I hope you didn't wait too long."

"Oh no. Only an hour and a half," he said, a little of his anger at being stood up returning.

"Oh. I feel terrible." She gave him a devilish smile and put a hand just above his left knee. "Maybe I can make it up to you."

He smiled. "Maybe I'll let you."

"I was on my way to meet you, but — well, it's sort of a long story. Where do you want to go?"

"I don't know. We don't have much choice, do we? Around here, you can either drive through town or drive through the hills."

"Let's drive through town and then through the hills," she said.

"Okay. I'm game." He scooted down in the seat. The leather felt smooth and cold. The car hummed softly as she pointed it down the sloping road toward town. The heater was turned on high. The warm air blowing up at him made him feel comfortable, happy, even a little drowsy.

"Tell me your long story," he said, not letting her off the hook.

She frowned and bit her lower lip. With her blonde hair flowing free to her shoulders and in that old-fashioned woolly poncho, she really did look like someone from another time. There was something sad about her, he suddenly thought. Then he realized it was probably his emotional roller coaster plunging over another steep hill. Why was he going up and down like that?

"I don't want to," she said, a bit annoyed.

"I'll force you to," he said, teasing.

"How will you do that?"

"I'll tickle you."

She smiled. "I'm not ticklish."

"Everyone is ticklish — somewhere," he said, trying to make it sound dirty.

"I'm not," she said, still smiling. "*Ohhh!*"

She swerved the car. It hit a bump and bounced over a ditch. She pulled the wheel back, and got them back on the road.

"It was an animal," she said. "It ran right under the tires. Yuck!"

Kerry's heart was pounding. "Forget about the tickling," he said. "I'm not doing any tickling while you're driving. Are you okay?"

"Yeah. I guess so." She leaned forward, staring intently out at the dark road. There were no streetlights in this section of the hills, and the road curved steeply as it made its way down toward town. "Did you see it? What was it?"

"It felt like an elephant," he said. "Maybe we should go somewhere. Maybe you don't want to spend the whole evening behind the wheel."

"No," she protested quickly. "No. Really.

I like to drive. I'd rather just stay in the car tonight and talk. I — well, maybe I will tell you why I didn't meet you this afternoon. I don't know. I can't decide."

"Sounds pretty heavy," he said. She hit another bump. He felt the tires skid over the pebbly asphalt. "Hey, slow down."

"Oh. Sorry. Gee. I was doing sixty-five. It doesn't feel like it in this car." She suddenly seemed very nervous. She peered into the rearview mirror. It was black.

"You must think I've been acting a little . . . weird . . . lately," she said, easing her foot off the gas. "Well, I mean, you don't really know me or anything. So maybe you think I'm just weird. But. . . ."

"That's it," Kerry said. "That's what I think."

He meant it as a joke, but she took it seriously. "Well, I don't blame you. I have been a little strange-o. But I — you see, there's a reason. I wasn't going to tell you about it. I mean, you've got enough problems."

"That's an understatement," he said.

"I don't know if it's fair of me to add any more. But I also don't want you to think I'm nuts or something. There *is* a reason why I've — I mean, why I didn't show up and why — "

She was silent for a long moment. They stopped at the traffic light at the bottom of the hill. There were no cars around, but they waited for the long red light to change. Then she started moving slowly. The road was flat and straight now. The wooded hills gave way to neat, orderly suburban houses.

"Well, I realize this is going to make me sound even more nuts . . ." she said, staring straight ahead, lowering her voice until it was nearly a whisper. "But I know I'm not. I know this is true. It's just that — "

"What is it?" Kerry asked impatiently. He was immediately sorry he hadn't covered his impatience. He could see that she was really upset and finding it difficult to tell him the reason.

"Well . . . I think someone's been following me. I mean, I *know* it."

They turned the corner onto Wellmore and drove past the elementary school. All of the lights were on, but the school was deserted.

"Why?" Kerry asked. "Who would follow you?"

"I don't know why," she said. Then she hesitated for a long time. "But I think I know who. . . ."

"Well, come on," he said impatiently. "Who?"

She turned her head to look him in the eye. "Donald. Your brother Donald."

The car bumped against the curve, narrowly missing a parked car. "Mandy — watch the road!" he cried.

"Sorry," she said, frowning, turning the wheel hard to the left.

"Why would my brother be following *you*?" Kerry asked. As he asked the question, Donald's voice on the phone came back to him. *"Be careful. I'm coming."*

"I *told* you — I don't know why," she said shrilly.

"Be careful. I'm coming."

Why on earth would Donald be following Mandy? Was he coming after both of them?

"This is getting too bizarre," Kerry said.

"I knew you'd think I'm nuts," she said dejectedly. She turned onto Sycamore.

"I don't think you're nuts," he said. "I think the world is nuts. Donald called me tonight and said — " Then he stopped. A thought burst into his mind. "Hey — how do *you* know my brother Donald?"

The question seemed to fluster her. She stared straight out the windshield, squinting her deep blue eyes as an oncoming car cast its yellow headlights at them. "I didn't say I knew your brother . . ." she said finally. "I just said he was following me. At least, I think he is following me."

Her answer didn't really satisfy him. He started to repeat his question. Then he realized they were driving past the house on Sycamore. The house he had thought was hers. Amanda's house.

Was she deliberately slowing down as they drove past the house?

No.

It couldn't be possible.

Then why was she driving so slowly? And why did she have that weird, distant smile on her face?

He glanced at the house, completely dark, completely deserted-looking. He knew the sad couple was inside. He saw their faces again, their looks of horror when they recognized him. "Oh. . . ."

"Why, Kerry — you got so pale. What's the matter?"

Was she mocking him? Was she being sarcastic?

No.

Stop it, Kerry, he told himself.

He was starting to be suspicious of *everyone*. He couldn't let that happen. He *couldn't*.

She turned right onto Hickory. The school was a few blocks down. "Nothing," he told her. "I'm okay."

The sad faces of Amanda's parents stayed with him. Why had she driven down Sycamore?

"That's why I disappeared for a while at the dance Sunday night," she said, breaking into his morbid thoughts. "I thought I saw Donald in the gym."

"But — that's impossible!" Kerry cried. But he realized it wasn't impossible.

"Then I thought he was watching us in the parking lot. That's why I ran for the bus."

"You saw him there? You actually saw him there?" Kerry asked, not wanting to believe any of it.

"Well . . . I didn't really see him . . . only his shadow." She shook her shoulders, a violent shiver. It made him feel bad that he was questioning her so suspiciously.

"When I went into town to meet you this afternoon, I saw the same shadow," she said. "I turned around, but there was no one there. I guess he didn't want me to see him. But I knew he was there. I knew." She bit her purple lips nervously.

"So you were at the restaurant? You were at Phil's?"

"Outside it. But he was right behind me. I ran. I got back into the car. I had to get away from him. I was so *scared*. . . ." Her shoulders began to shake violently up and down. He put a hand on her shoulder to calm her.

"Let's stop talking about it now," he said softly, soothingly. "Drive up into the South Hills. We'll park by the Point and talk."

"Talk? At the Point?" She gave him a sly smile.

"Yeah, talk," he said. "For a while, anyway." He laughed.

But he didn't really feel like laughing. They rode in silence up through the low hills. The moon was completely covered by clouds now. Even though it was still early, there were few cars on the road.

After a while, the silence began to make him feel uncomfortable.

Everything was making him uncomfortable tonight. He struggled to think of something to say, a new subject, something different to talk about.

He squinted. The car coming toward them had its brights on. The bright white beams of light were blinding against the deep black of the night.

"I ran into Margo in town. She said she didn't know you," he said.

Why had he said it? He wasn't going to mention it. It had just slipped out in his eagerness to say something.

"Hey — Mandy! No! Look out!"

She swerved the car toward the center of the road — into the path of the oncoming car. . . .

Chapter 15

The headlights burned into his eyes until all he could see was a shadowless glare of white. He heard the crunch of metal against metal, the shattering and cracking of glass.

Then he felt the jolt.

The impact threw him hard against the side of the car. The white glare became black, then flared white again.

A stab of pain crossed the side of his head. He cried out.

For some reason, there was a second jolt, a second slam against the hard car side, a second stab of pain.

He heard the steady whir of a tire spinning in the air. He heard glass, pieces of glass hitting the road, cracking.

He heard quiet sobs.

The side of his head felt wet, warm wetness. Blood?

He opened his eyes. The headlights were still in his eyes. Would he ever see again? Would he have the blinding whiteness in his eyes forever?

He tried to speak, but he could only gasp. His throat felt tight and clogged. He coughed. He tried to cough his throat clear.

"Hey — "

He could speak.

The pain in his side spread around his body.

His head throbbed.

He reached a hand up. It was blood. His head was bleeding.

Shadows emerged. He began to see.

He tried to lean forward. The pain was too intense.

The shadows darkened. The night reappeared. He could see again. He could see that the car was tilted. Lights from the other car, the car they had collided with, threw a steady white light onto the front seat.

He looked over at the girl. She was leaning forward at a funny angle. He gasped. He choked. Her head had gone through the windshield.

He called her name. "Amanda."

He pulled her arm. He pulled her head back into the car.

Her wide eyes stared back at him sightlessly.

Her mouth fell open.

She was dead.

"No! No! No!"

Amanda was dead.

Donald. What about Donald?

"Donald?" He called to him.

"What?"

He leaned past the dead girl and saw his brother.

Donald shook his head.

He was alive.

His window, the window on the right side of the car, was open.

Donald stuck his head out the window, gasping for air, sucking in the cool night air.

Donald was alive.

"Donald," Kerry said, blood dripping down his head onto his neck.

"Yeah. I'm here."

"*Amanda* . . ." Kerry started to say. Donald didn't know yet. Donald didn't know that his girl friend was dead. Only Kerry knew. Only Kerry.

Kerry pushed at the wheel in front of him.

"Amanda," Donald said.

"She's dead," Kerry told him.

He heard the whir of the spinning tire.

"No," Donald said.

"She's dead," Kerry said through his throbbing pain, through the white glare that curtained his eyes again, through the blood, through the nausea that was rising from his stomach. "She's dead — and it's all my fault."

"Whew! That was a close one," Mandy said.

She had pulled over and stopped by the side of the road.

"I don't know what happened. I guess my hand just slipped on the wheel."

Kerry waited for his heart to stop pounding, waited for the white glare to fade from his eyes. He was sweating, he realized, a cold, wet sweat. His clothing felt drenched.

"Lucky that guy swerved in time. We would've bought it," Mandy said, shaking her head. "Are you okay?"

Kerry didn't answer her.

He had seen it all. He had seen it in the glare of the oncoming headlights.

His memory had come back.

That night, that dreadful night of horror had come back.

"Kerry — what's the matter? Are you okay?"

Mandy's voice was far, far away.

It was a year ago. Amanda, Donald, and he were riding in the hills. He saw it all. He remembered it. He knew it.

They crashed, collided head-on with a big Buick.

The Buick had overturned. He remembered the sound of its tires whirring in the air.

Donald was okay, just stunned.

He had been cut. But not badly. He had a concussion.

And Amanda. Amanda . . . was . . . dead.

"Oh my god — no!" Kerry screamed at the top of his lungs.

Mandy shrieked, reached forward, grabbed him by the shoulders. "Kerry — what? What? We're okay. We're okay. We didn't crash!" she cried.

Amanda was dead. He saw it now. He saw it so clearly.

He saw it all. He heard it. He smelled it. Smelled the blood, the burning rubber, smelled the horror.

Amanda was dead — and it was all his fault.

He saw it so clearly, so clearly his side ached and his head throbbed, and he felt it all over again.

It was all his fault — *because he was the driver.*

He slowly became aware that Mandy was shaking him by the shoulders. She can shake me, but she can't shake away the memories, he thought.

"Kerry — come on. It's okay, Kerry. Please! It's okay. Stop — you're scaring me!"

"Mandy . . . you can stop . . . stop shaking me." He pulled himself up in the smooth leather seat. He looked around. The moon reappeared above them, pale and full, reassuring somehow.

There was no one around.

The other driver had yelled something out his window, shook his fist at Mandy, and had roared away.

"Kerry — you scared me," Mandy said, sounding cross. "We only had a close call, y'know. You don't have to go into shock."

"Sorry," he muttered. How could he explain to her what had just happened? How could he tell her that an entire section of his life, a terrifying, heartbreaking section that had been missing for more than a year, had just come back to him? He couldn't. No way.

"Mandy, some day . . ." he said. He tried not to sound too dramatic. "Some day I'll tell you what just happened to me. It's a long, long story — and not a happy one. But now, I think we'd better skip the Point. I'm not going to be very good company. I think we'd better call it a night."

"You want me to take you home?" She pouted again. But her eyes, those clear blue eyes, were filled with sympathy. She seemed to understand. "Okay," she said softly, patting his hand. "I'm really a very good driver. I don't understand — "

"I really can't explain now. It wasn't that." He suddenly felt weary, too weary to talk. He rested his head in his hands.

They drove back through town. They didn't say much. The car hummed quietly. Trees bent and rustled in the strong autumn wind.

He looked up. To his surprise, she had turned back onto Sycamore Street. "Hey, Mandy — " They were driving slowly past Amanda's house.

He remembered the house clearly now, remembered Amanda's parents, remembered hanging out in the basement rec room with Amanda and Donald, remembered everything, a flood of memories that took place inside this house.

"What?"

"Why are we — what are we doing on Sycamore?" Was she doing this to him deliberately? It wasn't possible — was it?

"I don't know. This is the way I always go. What street should I take?" She seemed totally innocent. Kerry felt terribly guilty for suspecting her.

Guilty.

He had a year of feeling guilty to catch up on.

He had been the driver. He had killed Amanda.

He had killed Donald's girl friend.

No wonder he had wiped the memory from his mind, shut it away for an entire year.

No wonder. . . .

No wonder Donald was coming to get him now.

"Be careful. I'm coming."

"You should take Edgemont. It's faster," he snapped at Mandy.

She looked startled. "Sorry. I didn't realize you were in such a big hurry to be rid of me." She stared straight ahead, not looking at him.

"That's not what I meant."

They rode the rest of the way without speaking. Every few minutes, he'd lift his head from his hands and look over at her. She looked so pretty. It was nice to have one pretty thing, one nice thing happening in his life.

But what was that expression on her face?

Why was she driving with that smile, that pleased smile? What was she so *pleased* about?

Chapter 16

He went right up to his room and tried to go to sleep. But he was wide awake. He stared at the shifting shadows of tree branches cast by the moon onto his low ceiling, shadows that beckoned, shadows that disturbed the night's stillness and made Kerry feel as if he were moving beneath them, moving through the year he had misplaced.

He remembered the night clearly now, also a breezy night of shifting shadows. He remembered the three of them hanging out in Amanda's rec room, Donald lying on the billiards table while Kerry and Amanda had to shoot around him. Amanda's mom brought them tall glasses of iced-tea. No — lemonade. It was bitter, terribly bitter, but they drank it anyway, making hilarious faces, trying to outgross each other. No, wait. Donald poured his into the rubber tree plant. That's right.

Then they went for a drive up in the South Hills. Whose idea was it, anyway? Donald's?

No, Amanda's. She always wanted to get away from home.

They were so happy, so silly. Donald and Amanda never seemed to mind if Kerry tagged along. At least, Kerry never noticed it. That made him very happy. It always made him happy to be with Donald, doing things that Donald did.

So they went for a drive. Kerry asked if he could drive. He was only fifteen, not old enough. But sometimes Donald let him drive, just for laughs.

Just for laughs.

Ha.

Donald pulled over. Amanda protested. He teased her. He got out of the car. Walked across the hood, doing a balancing act like he was on a high wire. Kerry got behind the wheel. Donald took Kerry's place, riding shotgun.

Donald took Kerry's place.

Donald was sent away — but Kerry wasn't. Donald took Kerry's place. But Kerry was the driver. Why wasn't Kerry sent away? Why was Donald the one who got punished?

Lying in bed, staring up at the twisting shadows, Kerry realized there was still a piece missing, still a part he didn't remember.

Was that why Donald was coming after him now? Because the wrong brother got punished for the crime?

Kerry got behind the wheel. It was dark in the hills and he was going too fast. He didn't really have control, but he was too scared to tell Donald. He didn't like to be laughed at — especially not by Donald, especially not in front of Amanda.

And then they crashed.

And Amanda died.

Blood all over.

He pulled her head back into the car and saw her eyes.

Her eyes. They looked so surprised.

And then he screamed.

And then. . . .

The piece was missing. What happened then?

What happened *next*?

"When'd you get in last night?" His father looked and sounded tired. He sucked on his coffee cup as if it was a matter of life or death.

"Early." Kerry didn't really feel like talking. Should he tell him that Donald had called? Probably. But he just didn't have the strength.

"You and this Mandy getting pretty serious?"

Kerry looked up, surprised. His father usually didn't ask such personal questions. "No. Not really."

He poured milk over his cornflakes and sat down across from his father. "Dad, I'm starting to get my memory back." He hadn't intended to tell him this morning. Why did he start? "I can remember the accident, that whole night — most of it, anyway."

Lt. Hart put the coffee cup down gently. He put both hands on the edge of the table, grasping the table as if for support. "That's good, Kerry. Maybe you should go see Dr. Kessel after school."

Dr. Kessel. Kerry had seen her three times a week for nearly eight months after the accident. She was a nice lady, a good listener. He had forgotten all about her, shut her out of his mind. "Yeah, maybe," he said.

"It isn't going to be easy to deal with. She can help you," Lt. Hart said, still gripping the table, his white knuckles the only sign that he was nervous about what Kerry was telling him. "God knows I can't help much. I'm only a cop."

"It's a help to talk to you, Dad."

That embarrassed his father. He pushed himself up, groaning from the pain in his back. "I gotta get goin'. Take care. And go see Dr. Kessel."

"Yeah. Right. Bye."

Lt. Hart started out the door, then stopped. "The boys at the lab went over the car," he said with a frown. "They didn't find much, no prints or anything. The tires were cut with some sort of hunting knife. And the windows, a hammer of some kind was used on 'em, a soft hammer, like a mallet. Any of your friends walk around with a hunting knife and a mallet?"

Kerry smiled. "I'll keep an eye out."

"You do that. Any more weird phone calls?"

Should he tell him about Donald? No. Something kept him from saying it. "No. No calls."

"Musta been a wrong number, right?"

"Right, Dad."

Musta been a *lot* of wrong numbers.

The week went by quickly. It was a short week since there'd been no school on Monday. Kerry felt calmer, having talked to Dr. Kessel. She urged him to tell his father about Donald's phone call, but he hadn't done it. He kept expecting to see Donald every time he turned a corner, every time he returned home, but there was no trace of him.

He spoke to Mandy a few times on the phone. Each time she seemed preoccupied and eager to get off. He asked if she still thought she was being followed, and she said yes.

"Maybe you should call the police," Kerry had suggested.

"Oh, that's very helpful," she had replied angrily.

"Shall we do something this weekend?" he asked.

"Maybe." Her voice was flat, bored.

The phone rang once late at night. He picked it up, filled with the dread he had become accustomed to. But it was only a wrong number, someone asking for Carlos. "Thanks for calling," he had said, feeling relieved.

Friday night, everyone was going out but

him. "I'm gone," Sean said, giving him a wave, his overnight bag in his other hand.

"Where you going?" Kerry asked.

But Sean was out the door. "He's going to see that friend of his who lives upstate. You know, the one with the horses."

Kerry didn't know. Sean didn't tell him much about his friends. Sean didn't tell him much, period.

"Where's my cap?" his father grumbled. "Why can't I ever find my cap?"

"Maybe you should have two caps," Kerry suggested. "You'd stand a better chance that way."

"A cop with *two* caps. That would shake up the whole department," his father chuckled. "It would be a major advance in police science."

He searched the living room until he found it, tucked between the cushions on the worn green sofa. He placed it carefully on his head and started to the door.

"Hey, Dad — "

"Yeah?"

"Something I didn't tell you," Kerry said softly.

"You had that look on your face," Lt. Hart said, coming back into the room, leaning on the sofa back.

"Donald called a few days ago."

Lt. Hart didn't look surprised, didn't change his blank expression. "I thought he might. What'd he say?"

"I didn't give him a chance," Kerry admitted, embarrassed. "I got so nervous, I accidentally hung up on him."

"And he didn't call back?"

"No. Huh-uh."

"So what'd he say?" his father repeated, looking into Kerry's eyes, trying to find more of the story there, just like a cop.

"He said, 'Be careful. I'm coming.' " Kerry shrugged.

His father finally showed some emotion. He turned his thin, white lips down in a frown and shook his head sadly. "I was afraid of this," he said, so quietly Kerry could barely hear him. "All those months in the hospital. . . ."

Kerry couldn't decide whether to tell him about Mandy and her feeling that Donald was following her. He decided not to. Why get her involved?

"Listen, Ker." Lt. Hart was thinking hard. "I really don't want to leave you alone here tonight."

"Why, Dad? You don't think that Donald wants to . . . hurt me . . . do you?" Kerry said, finding it hard to even say those unthinkable words. *His own brother?*

"I don't know. I really don't," Lt. Hart said, fiddling with the brim of his cap. "You said you got your memory back. Do you remember what happened after the accident?"

Kerry stared back at his father.

After the accident?

No.

Nothing.

"Dad, tell me," he said finally. "You've got to now. You've got no choice."

Lt. Hart considered this for a long time, staring down at the green couch, shaking his head. When he looked up, he looked a hundred years old.

"Kerry — *your brother tried to kill you.*"

"After the accident, Donald went berserk," Lt. Hart said in a flat, emotionless policeman's tone. "He just lost control, I guess. When we came on the scene, he had dragged you out of the car. He was shaking you, choking you, screaming at the top of his lungs.

"That's why Donald was sent away, Kerry. It took three men to pull him off you. Three men."

"But he didn't know what he was doing, right?" Kerry said through his shock, through his sorrow.

The question seemed to catch his father by surprise. "Well . . . I guess you could say that. He was definitely out of his mind."

"So he didn't really know what he was doing. He didn't really know it was me or anything, right?"

"The hatred was still there, Kerry. The fury was still there. His hands were around your throat."

Kerry stared at his father. There didn't seem to be anything more to say.

He had it now. The missing piece. He didn't want it. But he had it.

"I didn't want to tell you," Lt. Hart said,

still gripping the back of the sofa. "I never wanted to tell you." They stared at each other for a long while. The room seemed to grow dark even though the lights were on.

"I've gotta go," Lt. Hart said finally. "I don't want to leave you here tonight. But I have no choice. Listen, Ker, lock all the doors after I leave. I'm gonna call McCarty and see that a patrol car goes by here every fifteen minutes. The house will be under watch. You should be okay if Donald — if Donald — "

"I'll be okay," Kerry said, his voice nearly a whisper.

"If you hear or see anything, call the station immediately, hear?"

"Right, Dad."

"And listen — don't go out. I mean that. Stay here. Stay locked up. Your brother may not mean you any harm. But we don't know for sure. I'll make sure that patrol car is around here all the time. So you just stay put, okay?"

"Okay, Dad," Kerry said, annoyed. "I'll be fine. Fine. I'll pull a Sean tonight. I'll lie here and watch some old sitcoms."

"You do that," Lt. Hart said. He finally let go of the sofa. He turned and disappeared out the front door. "Hey — lock up!" he called from outside.

Shaking his head, Kerry walked to the front door and locked it. Then he walked through the kitchen and locked the back door. Somehow the fact that his father was more upset than he was cheered him. He knew it would be a long night. He knew he'd jump every time a twig cracked outside the house. But he just couldn't picture it.

He just couldn't picture his brother coming back to kill him.

Not Donald.

Not good-natured, fun-loving Donald. Not his *brother*.

Still. . . . He locked the windows and pulled the shades.

The back of his neck felt tight and stiff. He felt a little dizzy. He realized his heart was pounding. Yes, it would be a long night.

What was that noise?

Something scrabbled across the roof.

A squirrel?

He held his breath and listened.

Silence.

I'd better put on some music or something, he thought. I need some noise around here.

Something squeaked.

He jumped. It was just the floor beneath his sneakers.

Oh boy, was it going to be a long night!

When the phone rang, he nearly jumped *out* of his sneakers!

His throat tightened. He didn't know if he could answer it.

Was it Donald? Was it a call from the girl who was threatening to break his bones?

He decided not to answer it.

It rang and rang.

He couldn't keep to his resolve. He picked it up.

"Kerry — it's me. Mandy."

"Oh, hi, Mandy. I'm so glad — "

"Kerry, you've got to help me. I'm so frightened. It's Donald. I think he's here — in the house. Please, Kerry. *Please!*"

Chapter 17

Her voice still echoed in his ear for a long time after he had hung up. "I can't stay here," she had said, out of breath, talking in a terrified whisper. "I locked him in the basement. I've got to get away. I'll be right over."

And then she had hung up before he could say a word.

Had she hung up? Or had the line been cut?

Of course she hung up, he told himself. Don't start imagining things. Don't start making it worse. How could it be worse?

He replaced the receiver on the phone, but he didn't move. He had to think, had to clear his head, had to figure out the best thing to do. At first, he was happy Mandy was on her way over to his house. He needed the company. And he liked the idea of coming to her rescue.

But would Mandy be any safer with him? What could the two of them do against

Donald if he really was a raging, dangerous lunatic out to get her — or them?

"Be careful. I'm coming."

And why was Donald chasing after Mandy?

What was her connection to Donald?

The answer came to Kerry in a flash, a sudden realization that filled him with dread. She had *no* connection to Donald. Her only connection to Donald was — Kerry.

Donald was following Mandy because of *Kerry.*

Donald was out to get Mandy because of *Kerry.*

Kerry had killed Donald's girl friend. And now Donald had come back — had escaped from a *mental hospital* — and had come back to kill Kerry's girl friend!

Something clattered against the kitchen window, and Kerry's heart leaped into his throat. "Aggh!" he cried aloud, then realized it was probably just an acorn dropping off the tree in the back or a clump of dried leaves.

He walked to the refrigerator on shaky legs and got a Coke. He pulled open the can and took a long drink, telling himself to calm down. How can I calm down when it's all my fault? came the answer.

Now he felt terribly guilty for the suspicions he had begun to have about Mandy. When she had driven twice past the house on Sycamore Street, it had crossed his mind that she was taking that route deliberately. And then there had been that odd, pleased smile, so out of place, so mysterious, that smile he had caught on her face the night he regained his memory.

But how ridiculous to suspect her. All along, he should've suspected *himself*. Poor Mandy. She was in danger because of him, because of something he had done more than a year before she met him.

He made up his mind to protect her.

But how? What could he do?

He was startled from his thoughts by insistent pounding on the front door. He ran to the door, began to turn the knob — then hesitated. What if it wasn't Mandy?

"Who's there?"

"It's me — Mandy. Where were you? I've been knocking on the door for nearly a minute!"

He pulled open the door. "I'm sorry. I was — "

She threw her arms around him and buried her face in his neck. "Kerry, I'm so glad, so glad. Thank you," she said. Her face felt hot against his neck. He returned her hug.

If she only knew, if she only knew the truth, he told himself, she wouldn't be thanking me.

"Everything'll be okay," he said unconvincingly. He liked having her so close to him, pressing against him like this. But he could feel her fear, feel the desperation in her touch, and it only increased his feelings of guilt.

She pulled away suddenly. "Quick," she said, her eyes darting around the small living room. "We can't stay here. He'll be after us."

"No," he said, holding her shoulders. "We have to stay. We'll be safe here."

"We'll be sitting ducks here," she said, her voice suddenly hard. "We have to get far away, some place he doesn't know, some place where he won't be able to find us."

"I promised my dad," Kerry said, walking to the sofa, wanting to be away from the window. "He said to stay here."

"No. No. We can't." Her eyes were wild with fear. Fear that was all his fault. She was pleading with him now. "There's a cabin," she said, following him to the sofa. "It's in Granger Forest. Relatives of mine own it. But they're not there now. I have a key. Kerry, listen to me. We'll be safe there. He won't find us."

"No, I can't—" Kerry started. But he realized she was right. They would be safer away from the house, this house Donald knew so well. He had to try to protect her. It was his fault Donald was chasing her. He had to do something—even if it meant going against his father's wishes.

"Okay," he said. "You're right. Let's go."

She hugged him again. She seemed so grateful, so desperate. "We'll be safer . . ." she whispered in his ear, her breath hot against his face, "and we'll be together." Her lips brushed his cheek.

"I — I'll — uh — call my dad," he stammered. "Then we'll go."

"Hurry. Please," she said, her voice tiny like a little girl's.

"Dad won't like it," he said, "but he'll realize it's the safest plan." He picked up the receiver and started to dial. "Hey!" he cried in surprise. "No dial tone. It's silent. Dead." The surprise turned to fear.

"Oh my god!" she cried. "We've got to get out of here!"

"I'll be back in two seconds," he said, dropping the dead phone receiver to the floor. He ran upstairs and pulled his backpack from the closet. He stuffed a few shirts and other clothes into it, grabbing them from his dresser drawer without looking. Then he came running down the steps. "Okay. Let's make tracks."

"You sound like a bad movie," she said.

"I wish it was a movie," he muttered, as they stepped outside.

The night was colder than he had thought. His breath steamed, and he shivered from the surprise chill. Mandy opened the trunk to the Firebird. "Throw your pack in here," she said, her eyes surveying the trees warily. She was shivering, too.

The trunk was filled with camping gear, a canvas tent, fishing rods, a tackle box, an overnight bag, and a long wooden mallet.

Kerry felt a sinking feeling in his stomach. "Mandy!" he called. She was already climbing into the driver's seat.

"What? Hurry, will you?"

"Mandy — this mallet. What's it for?"

"What?" Frowning, she came running to the back of the car. "What's the problem?"

"What's this mallet for?"

"I didn't put it there. It's my dad's. You know, for pounding in tent pegs. Come on, Kerry. What's the matter with you? Let's go!"

Again, the guilty feelings. Why was he so suspicious? How could he suspect this poor, frightened girl? Shaking his head, he climbed in beside her. She started the car and floored it, and they sped off down the hill.

"Maybe we'll use the mallet," she said suddenly, eyes on the curving road. "We'll pitch a tent in the woods. That'll be romantic."

"And cold," he said, still shivering.

"I'll keep you warm," she whispered, squeezing his hand and giving him a sexy smile. She wore an oversized gray sweat shirt over jeans. He realized it was the first time he had seen her dressed like a normal person. He smiled back. She looked terrific. He was beginning to warm up to the idea of being out in the woods in a cabin alone with her.

The highway became a road. The road became a gravel path. The gravel gave way to dirt. "It's right up there, hidden behind the tall pine trees," she said, her bright headlights cutting through the dark, frosty air, illuminating a thick tangle of pines and oaks and white-barked cedars that seemed to jump out at the car.

The cold wind howled. Tree branches bent and shuddered. Fat, brown leaves blew up against the windshield as they made their way slowly up the twisting dirt road toward the hidden cabin. "Are you sure you know where you're going?" Kerry said.

"No," she said. She smiled. "Does it really matter?" She seemed less nervous out here, surrounded by the shifting, blowing darkness. She smiled easily again, and her voice had regained its purr. "Kerry, you look so cold."

"I didn't realize. I should've brought my — "

"We'll get a roaring fire going in the fireplace. We'll be cozy and warm before you know it." She dropped a hand to his thigh and let it rest there for a while. "I'll make you glad you rescued me," she said softly, her eyes on the narrow, twisting path ahead.

Kerry smiled.

This may turn out to be a memorable weekend, he told himself.

Suddenly, she stopped the car. "We're here."

She climbed out of the car and walked up to the cabin door. He stood at the car and watched her struggle with the key. Finally, she managed to get the door open. She disappeared inside, and a few seconds later, a bright lamp went on outside the cabin door and a few lights inside came to life.

The cabin was surrounded by tall weeds and overgrown grass that was more than knee-high. It appeared no one had tended to it in quite a long while. In the light, Kerry could see that it was pretty large, two or three bedrooms probably, built of logs and wide slats of pine, weathered and very run-down looking. One of the side windows was cracked and had been covered with a sheet. A four-legged animal of some sort, probably a raccoon or a mole, scampered away as Kerry walked up to the front door. The animal startled him, and he nearly tripped over a clump of tangled weeds.

"It looks pretty good inside," Mandy said, appearing suddenly at the doorway, looking pale, almost ghostly in the yellow light from the cabin lamp. "There's even some canned food in the pantry. Nothing great, but we won't starve."

Kerry shivered. "Let's unpack the trunk," he said. "I'm freezing." He couldn't stop shivering now. Was it just the cold?

She leaned over and gave him a quick, warm kiss on the cheek. "I know some good ways to warm you up," she said, teasing. Before he could react, she ran to the car trunk and reached into her jeans pocket for the key. He walked carefully through the overgrown weeds to help her unload.

"What was that?" she cried, grabbing his arm tightly. They heard footsteps, crunching, a twig cracking a few hundred yards away in the trees.

"Animals, I guess," Kerry said, trying to hide his own fear. "It's *their* forest, you know."

"But do they have to walk around so loudly?" she asked, lifting her suitcase from the trunk.

After they got all of their belongings inside, Kerry looked for the phone. "I've got to reach my dad," he told her. "Otherwise he'll have the entire police force going nuts." The kitchen was small but fully equipped with an electric stove and oven, a refrigerator, even a dishwasher. It was wallpapered, a hideous yellow and pink flower design, faded and peeling at the ceiling corners.

The phone was an old-fashioned black one at the corner of the stained Formica kitchen counter. Kerry picked it up and began to dial. Silence. The phone was dead. "No dial tone," he told her.

"Oh, gee," she said, looking very concerned. "I'm sorry. They probably have it turned off. No one uses the cabin much after the summer."

Kerry shivered. "It's almost as cold inside as out," he said angrily. "Is there a town nearby, someplace I can call from?"

She shrugged. "I don't know. I'm a tourist here, too, y'know."

Kerry began to pace back and forth in the tiny kitchen. "*Now* what am I going to do?" he asked.

"You're going to go get firewood so we can warm this place up," Mandy said softly, trying to soothe him. "We'll get a nice fire going, and I'll make us big, steaming cups of hot chocolate."

"That sounds okay," he said, still thinking about how he was going to call his dad.

"It'll be more than okay. You'll see," she purred. "Then we'll stay up all night, telling each other our problems and our life stories, and . . . other stuff."

He smiled despite his mood. "That 'other stuff' sounds interesting," he said.

She pushed him toward the door. "There's a small shed out in back," she told him. "There always used to be a big pile of firewood next to the shed. Go see. Bring back a lot. It's a big fireplace. And I love a big fire."

He clumped outside. The cold stung his face. Tall weeds brushed his jeans as he made his way around the cabin, sending small animals scurrying, his socks wet from the frost, turning his left ankle in a small hole as he tried to walk. There was no light in the back. He waited for his eyes to adjust. He could make out the dark outline of a low shed and he headed toward it. An animal howled in the distance, another picking up its cry.

What am I doing here? he asked himself. A few hours ago, I was in my warm house in front of the TV, safe and —

Well . . . he wasn't safe.

Now, at least, he was with Mandy. And far away from Donald.

He took a deep breath. The air was cold but

fresh. Things could be worse, he thought. If only he could reach his dad. . . .

There was a stack of firewood, neatly cut and piled by the side of the shed. He cradled four logs in his arms and started to the cabin with them. They were frost-covered but they would burn. He wondered if there was any kindling.

Mandy was at the stove, stirring a pot with a big wooden spoon. He stumbled at the entrance, nearly spilling the logs across the kitchen floor. "Very gracefully done," she said, and laughed. "I get the feeling you're not the outdoors type."

"Oh, I go outdoors all the time," Kerry said, brightening a little at her good humor. "Whenever I'm not indoors, I'm usually outdoors."

"Go put the logs in the fireplace," she said in a mock scolding tone. "If that's the level of conversation we're going to have, it's gonna be a long night!" She laughed again.

"You certainly got in a good mood," he said.

The remark seemed to startle her. "Oh. Well . . . I . . . I guess it's being with you." She turned back to her stirring.

The other room was used as a living and a dining room. The wide fireplace, which had been swept clean and didn't appear to have been used recently, took up most of the far wall. A small dining room table of painted oak stood in front of the fire, with four wooden chairs around it. A couch with one torn cushion stood against one wall. A moose head with only one antler was hung at a tilt above the couch.

Not the most luxurious, Kerry told himself. If there's no kindling, I can always use the dining room chairs — or the moose head.

But he found a basket of sticks to the right of the fireplace, and he set to work building the fire. A few moments later, he stepped back proudly. A few of the sticks had caught fire. The fireplace soon began to crackle and glow. The logs sizzled, then smoked, then finally low flames began to nip and flare around the edges.

"Not exactly a roaring blaze," Mandy said, smiling, setting down two large gray mugs on the small dining room table in front of the fire.

"Give it time, give it time," Kerry said. "In a few minutes, I promise, this place will be a raging inferno!"

Again, Mandy seemed startled by his remark. She gave him a curious look, then quickly tried to cover it with a smile. "Sit down," she said, pointing to his mug, which she had placed across from her on the table. "Drink this. It will warm you."

"Smells great," Kerry said, sitting down. The chair was hard and cold. He looked to the fire. "Not bad. It's getting there," he said.

"It'll warm the entire room," she said. "Once it gets going." She sipped her hot chocolate. "Mmmmm . . . nice and hot."

Kerry sipped his. It burned his tongue, but he didn't mind. He just wanted to get warm. "Good," he said. They looked at each other across the table. He suddenly felt very shy. I don't believe it, he thought to himself. I'm going to spend the night with this girl! He took another hot gulp of the chocolaty drink.

"It . . . it's going to be a very nice fire," Mandy said, staring at the flickering orange and yellow flames. Something popped, shooting bright red sparks against the fireplace screen. "This is just how I imagined it."

Kerry took a long drink of hot chocolate. He was beginning to feel warmer. "Imagined what?" he said quietly, becoming hypnotized by the flickering flames and their darting shadows.

"What?"

"You said this is exactly how you imagined it."

"I did?" She seemed embarrassed.

"Yes, you did," Kerry insisted.

"I don't really know what I meant. Fires always make me a bit dreamy," she said, reaching across the table and taking his hand. "It's such a shame, Kerry."

She was really confusing him now. *What* was a shame?

"Are you feeling okay?" he asked.

"Sure," she said, still holding his hand. "Now that you're here with me. Everything's going to be fine. Are *you* okay?"

"Yeah, I guess," he said. His back itched. He suddenly felt *too* warm. "That fire gives off a lot of heat, doesn't it?" he said, pulling off his sweater and tossing it onto the couch. He took another long sip of the hot chocolate.

"I told you I'd get you nice and warm," she said softly.

"Good hot chocolate," he said, thinking about her hand, which still held onto his.

"It's an old family recipe," she said. "Right from an envelope."

"You haven't told me much about your family," Kerry said, and he tried to cover a yawn with his hand.

"You don't want to hear about my family. You're yawning already," she teased, squeezing his hand.

"No. Really, I do." He yawned again. "I suddenly feel so sleepy. I'm sorry. I guess it's the change from being so cold to being so . . . warm. Are you hot, too?"

She laughed. "Am I *hot*? Don't be crude. I thought you wanted to hear about my family."

His head felt heavy. It was hard to keep his eyes open. He looked into the fire, so warm, so silent, so peaceful. . . .

"You look so sleepy, poor baby," Mandy said. She leaned across the table, lowered her head, and kissed the back of his hand. "Poor, poor baby."

"I'm . . . not . . . really. . . ." Kerry's eyes closed. He struggled to open them. He could hear Mandy's voice. She was saying, "Poor, poor baby," over and over again, he thought. But she sounded miles away. Miles and miles. . . . The fire had turned gray. What happened to the flames? It was still burning hot, but he couldn't see the flames . . . only gray . . . only gray. . . . He was falling, falling into a gray sleep.

Catch me. Catch me, Mandy, he thought.

But she was miles and miles away. Poor baby.

He woke up slowly, groggily, his head as heavy as a rock. He saw that the fire had burned low, the blackened logs still hissing over gray ashes. His back ached. He realized he was still sitting at the small dining room table.

His head ached.

He tried to stand up.

But he couldn't.

The fact that he couldn't woke him up.

He saw that his hands were tied behind him with a thick coil of rope.

He tried to kick away from the chair.

But his ankles were tied together. And his feet were tied tightly to the chair legs.

"Poor baby," Mandy said, standing across the table. Her dark purple lips were spread wide across her pale face in a grin. Her pale blue eyes, normally so flat and unrevealing of any emotion, sparkled with life.

"Poor baby," she said. "You're awake."

Chapter 18

Wake up, Kerry. Wake up! This is the worst dream yet! he told himself.

"It's all perfectly real," Mandy said, reading his thoughts, enjoying his struggles to free himself. "Don't pull like that. You'll cut your wrists."

"Mandy — come off it! What's the big idea? What the hell do you think you're doing?"

"It's just the way I imagined it," she said, smiling. She raised her hands excitedly and tugged at the sides of her hair. "I can't believe it!"

"I can't either," Kerry said, still struggling. "Untie me. This isn't funny."

"Not funny? Of course, it's funny, Kerry dear. And it's going to get a lot funnier."

"What do you think you're doing? Could you just explain to me — "

"It's perfect! Perfect!" she said, clapping her hands. "I don't want to start. I just want to look at you like this. But I have to. I *have* to."

"Have to what?" Kerry screamed angrily.

"Why, finish what I've started," she said, as if the answer was obvious.

"How did you do this to me?" Kerry asked.

"I put a little white powder in your hot chocolate. How else? You're being very dumb, Kerry."

"Dumb? *I'm* being dumb? This is the dumbest thing I ever heard of! Mandy — untie me!"

"I'm sorry," she said, still smiling broadly. "I have to finish."

"Finish what? Are you going to explain to me?"

"It's taken so long, so long," she said dreamily, not hearing his yells of protest. "I've worked so hard. . . ."

"Worked? What? Let me go!" He gave the ropes a powerful tug, and then screamed as they cut into his skin. He slumped back in the chair. He decided not to struggle anymore. "This is a bad joke, Mandy. I know you like to think you're impulsive and weird and everything, but — "

"Weird?" Her eyes flared angrily and she stormed back and forth, staring furiously at him. "I'm not weird. Don't ever say I'm weird, Kerry. Don't ever say that!"

He had to laugh. "Okay. Fine. You're not weird. What's weird about taking a person out to a cabin in the forest, drugging him, and tying him to a chair? Perfectly normal."

"*Shut up!*" she screamed, spitting the words at him, her face suddenly reddening with hatred. "Do you want me to explain? Okay. Maybe *this* will explain the situation to you!"

She put her fingers to her nose and pinched her nose tight. Then in a harsh, distorted voice — a voice Kerry knew well — she said, "The toe bone's connected to the foot bone . . . the foot bone is connected to the ankle bone. . . ."

"*No!*" Kerry screamed. "It was *you*! You made all those phone calls!"

"Give the boy a gold star," she said quietly, her eyes narrowing to slits of hatred. She turned her back as if she couldn't bear to look at him anymore.

"But why, Mandy — why?"

"The ankle bone's connected to the leg bone . . . the leg bone's connected to the knee bone . . ." she said furiously, her voice distorted by hatred. She began to pace back and forth again, faster and faster. It was as if the excitement was too much for her to bear in one place.

"Mandy — everything else . . . the red paint in my locker . . . the slashed tires. . . ."

She laughed and turned to look at him. "You catch on quick, Kerry baby. Not quick enough, though."

He stared into her laughing face. She didn't look like the same person. Her eyes were wild. She had pulled her hair out at the sides so that it stood up as if electrified.

He tried to think of what to do, what to say to her to get her to release him. He had to get free. She looked crazy enough to do *anything*!

"Mandy," he said quietly. "Sit down. Tell me why you're angry. Let's discuss this like — "

She walked up to him and stuck her face right in front of his so that their noses touched. "The toe bone's connected to the knee bone . . . the knee bone's connected to the neck bone . . . the neck bone's connected to the broken bone. . . . Ha ha!"

She grabbed his head. He tried to turn away, but he couldn't. She pressed her lips against his, harder, harder, until he could feel the blood trickling down his chin. Then she stood up straight and slapped his face.

"Time to start," she said, sounding perfectly calm again.

"Mandy, please — "

She disappeared from his view. He strained against the ropes, but they held tight. When she reappeared, she was carrying the long wooden mallet. "Time to keep my promise," she said quietly, almost absentmindedly. She was there holding the mallet, yet Kerry could see that she was also somewhere else, her mind a million miles away.

"You're nuts! Nuts!" he screamed, regretting it immediately.

Anger flared in her eyes again. "Yell all

you want. I'll enjoy it," she said, and smiled a bitter smile. "Boy oh boy, will I enjoy it."

"I'm sorry," Kerry said desperately. "Really. I didn't mean it. Let's talk. Mandy, please. You and I, together, we can — "

"Yes. Together," she said softly. "But first I have to keep my promise."

"What on earth are you talking about? What promise?"

"To break every bone in your body." She raised the mallet to her shoulder. It was heavy and she had difficulty balancing it. "One by one, one by one. Every bone. Each and every one."

"But, Mandy — " Kerry could see that she was deadly serious. "Why? At least tell me why!"

She walked over to him again, the mallet balancing precariously on her narrow shoulder. She stared down at him, the almost irisless blue eyes burning into his, her face aflame, her hair wild about her head. "Kerry — you mean you don't know?"

"Know? Know what?"

There was a long, long pause.

And then she said, "Amanda was my sister!"

Chapter 19

"Amanda's — sister?" Kerry was practically shrieking. His heart pounded. Sweat poured down his forehead even though the fire had died and the room had chilled. "That's impossible! I don't remember — "

"You don't remember *much*, do you?" she screamed the words into his face. He tried to grab her, but of course he couldn't. She pulled back, her dark purple mouth twisted in hate. "It was so convenient for you not to remember, wasn't it, Kerry. But I remember! I remember everything!"

"It was an accident. I — "

"You seem to have a lot of accidents, poor baby. Oh, how my family suffered because of your *accident* — how *I* suffered. And you, you slime, you got off scot-free, didn't you. And *how* did you get off scot-free?"

"Scot-free? I — "

"Because your old man was a cop! You got off without even a trial. Well, trial time has come, Kerry baby. I vowed I'd get justice for my sister. I vowed I'd break every bone in your body, just the way you broke hers."

"Now listen, I'm sure that my father didn't do anything to — " Kerry realized she wasn't listening, she was beyond listening.

She dropped the mallet to the floor and knelt down in front of Kerry. He kicked at her, but his foot was tied too tightly to move. She grabbed his left leg.

"Hey — what are you — "

She pulled off his left shoe. Then she grabbed the other leg and pulled off his right shoe. Breathing heavily, she pulled off his socks, her fingernails scratching his legs as she pulled them down, and tossed them into the fireplace.

She stood up and retrieved the mallet. "Let's start with the toe bones and work up," she said quietly.

She raised the mallet.

"No," Kerry pleaded. "Please, no."

She cried out as she brought the mallet down with all her might.

This time the sound of the cracking bone was Kerry's.

He screamed, a howl that poured out of him, a howl that wouldn't stop. The pain started at the toes of his left foot and shot up his left side, pain that made him howl, pain that closed his eyes, that tightened every muscle, that paralyzed him until he was nothing, nothing but a howl, a terrified, agonized howl.

When he opened his eyes, she was raising the mallet again.

"Poor baby," she said emotionlessly. "Something bad happened to your toes. Let's see what we can do to the other foot. Okay?"

He couldn't talk, not even to plead with her. He couldn't move.

He closed his eyes as she raised the mallet off her shoulder.

The pain, the pain was overwhelming. His foot had become a throbbing, aching knot of pain. Now she was about to do the same to his other foot.

"What's wrong, Kerry?" she called in that mocking, falsely sympathetic voice. "Can't bear to look? Okay. Okay. You caught me in a good mood." She reached up over the sofa and with great effort pulled the one-antlered moose head off the wall. She ripped the head from the base and frantically scooped out hunks of stuffing.

"Noooo," Kerry managed to scream. His foot throbbed, but the pain had subsided enough for him to get his voice back. "Mandy, noooo — "

She jammed the moose head over Kerry's head and pulled it down over him. It smelled of mildew and decay. He gasped. He tried to hold his breath. He twisted his head from side to side, but the moose head was pulled down securely over him, burying him in darkness and its foul odor.

"You look adorable," she said. "I wish I

had a camera." She laughed. He could hear the scrape of the mallet against the wood floor as she picked it up.

He didn't have to see to know what she was about to do next. She was about to slam the mallet down on his other bare foot.

"The toe bone's connected to the head bone . . . the head bone's connected to the moose bone. . . ."

He could hear her singing through the disgusting animal head. He shut his eyes. He tried to hold his breath. He could feel a powerful wave of nausea rise up from his stomach.

"Okay, Kerry baby . . . here it comes," she said happily.

Chapter 20

His stomach churning, his head reeling, he waited in the darkness of the disgusting animal head, waited for the second explosion of pain.

Something crawled across his forehead. It's just sweat, just sweat, he told himself. But he knew it was an insect. The moose head was probably crawling with insects. He felt as if he was about to pass out, as if he was slipping, slipping away.

A loud crash revived him. It sounded like the door bursting open.

"No! Go away!" he heard Mandy yell.

He heard sounds of a scuffle, feet scraping against the wooden floor, bodies colliding with furniture. "Go away! Go *away*!" Mandy kept yelling, her voice a shriek in the distance on the other side of the odorous animal head.

Was it Donald? Had Donald caught up to them? Had Donald come to finish off the job she had started? He strained against the ropes with new desire to escape, but it was of no use.

Chairs overturned. The mallet clunked to the floor. The fireplace utensils clanged and clattered to the floor with a metallic crash. "Get away from me! Go away!"

"Stop it, Nancy! Just *stop*!" a masculine voice, out of breath from the struggle, cried out.

Was it Donald? He couldn't tell. The sound was muffled through the heavy moose head. His forehead itched like crazy. Hundreds of little feet were walking across it.

Nancy?

He couldn't have heard right.

"Let me finish!" Mandy was screaming. "Let me take care of him!"

"*I'll* take care of him!" the masculine voice insisted.

Yes . . . it sounded like Donald.

They were fighting over which one of them got to mallet him to a pulp.

Dishes crashed. Something heavy smashed against a window. He could hear the shatter of glass. More scuffling feet.

"Nancy — stop! *I'll* take care of him! Stop! I don't want to hurt you!"

"Get away! Get away! Get away!"

Then he heard her utter a cry of pain. He heard a body hit the floor.

Silence.

Silence.

Footsteps. Coming toward him.

Someone was standing in front of him. He could feel a warm presence.

He waited.

He wanted to cry out.

But he waited.

Someone was standing there, standing over him, watching him.

Someone lifted the moose head.

The light was blinding white. The air was cold against his hot, wet skin.

"Donald!" Kerry cried.

"Happy Halloween," Donald said quietly. He still held the moose head in one hand. In the other hand he held the mallet.

In the light of the cabin, his brother looked older. His eyes seemed to have narrowed, and they were circled with dark rings. He stood stooped, his head at a low angle, bone-thin, his blond hair cut short.

Donald stared down at him, the mallet at his side. He dropped the moose head to the floor and kicked it aside.

This is it, Kerry thought. Donald's big moment. He's waited a year for his revenge and now he's about to get it. Kerry looked away and saw Mandy lying face down in front of the fireplace.

He knocked her out of the way so he could get to me, Kerry thought. Donald raised the mallet. Kerry sucked in his breath.

Donald tossed the mallet aside.

"Looks like you've been leading an interesting life, Ker," he said, a smile slowly breaking across his face, crinkling his tired eyes.

"Donald, I'm — I'm sorry —" Kerry blurted out.

"*You're* sorry?" Donald said softly. "I'm the one who's sorry, Ker. I had no idea she'd go this far. Really. . . ."

"Is she — is she —" Kerry looked over at the unmoving body of Mandy.

"I gave her a light tap," Donald said. "She'll be okay." He knelt down and began to untie the ropes around Kerry's ankles. "My foot . . ." Kerry said. The throbbing pain was almost unbearable.

"Looks like you've got some broken toes," Donald said, untying the last knot. "I'm sorry. I tried to catch up with her. I tried to get to her in time. But each time she managed to get away." He began to rub Kerry's leg to get the circulation going.

"I don't get it," Kerry said, his head spinning.

"I wanted to catch her in a tranquil situation," Donald said, shaking his head. "I thought I could talk to her, reason with her. But I was wrong. I'm sorry, Ker. I'm real sorry. This was all my fault. I called you. I tried to warn you about her. But you hung up on me."

"It was an accident, Donald. I didn't mean to. I just — Why didn't you call back?"

Donald frowned. His eyes became sad slits. "I thought maybe you and Dad didn't want to hear from me. After I nearly killed you last year, I thought maybe you didn't want me bothering you. You see, I have a *lot* to be sorry about. So I tried to take care of it on my own. I tried to stop her without troubling anybody. I almost did, too. Almost."

He got one hand untied. Kerry tried to lift it, but the entire arm was tingly and numb. Donald went to work on the second hand.

"You mean that Mandy —" Kerry began, struggling to make sense of things.

"Her name isn't Mandy," Donald said, surprised. "She told you her name was Mandy? Man oh man." He whistled, a whistle of surprise he always whistled, a whistle Kerry hadn't heard in over a year. "That's what I used to call Amanda. Her name is Nancy. Nancy Kelly."

"I don't believe it," Kerry said, the feeling beginning to return to his arm. "Next you're gonna tell me that I'm not Kerry. I'm Murray Peterson from Nome, Alaska."

"Yeah, that's right," Donald said. "And I'm the Great Pumpkin."

Kerry grimaced as Donald untied the last tight knot around his wrist. He didn't even try to move the hand. The entire arm was numb.

"How can she be Amanda's sister if her name is Nancy Kelly?" Kerry asked.

"She isn't Amanda's sister," Donald told him with a bitter frown. "She only thinks she is."

"But she told me —" Kerry stopped. He

didn't know what to say. His mind was flooded with a million questions all at once.

"She thinks she's Amanda's sister," Donald said softly. "She really believes it. Nancy is a very sick girl. I didn't realize *how* sick, I guess. I should have stopped her sooner. I shouldn't have risked your getting hurt. I shouldn't have — "

"Shouldn't have *what*?" Kerry insisted.

"Shouldn't have told her the whole story, about me and Amanda, and you, and the accident. But what *else* was I going to talk about up in that hospital?"

"You mean she was there, too?" Kerry asked.

"Yeah, she's been there most of her life, poor kid. She's had several different identities, none of them her own. She hides in other people's lives. She becomes other people. I told her all about the accident, why I was in the hospital, everything. I even told her about this cabin that Amanda's parents own.

"She remembered everything," Donald continued. "She absorbed everything I told her. And I guess she just moved into the story, took a part for herself, became Amanda's sister. I was an idiot. I was lonely, so I talked to her. I told her too much.

"When she escaped from the hospital, I knew where she was going, what she was going to do. I *knew* it."

"So you decided to go after her?" Kerry asked, staring up at his brother.

"I knew I could talk to her, bring her back

safely," Donald replied, looking over at Nancy's unmoving body. "So I waited till the right moment and got away. It's okay. The doctors will understand when I explain. I was gonna be released in a few days anyway. So . . . I came after her. I knew she'd be staying with a friend who lives near town. I was determined to reason with her, to bring her back safely. The whole thing was my fault.

"I almost got to her tonight, Ker. But she heard me and locked me in the basement. . . ."

As Donald continued his explanation, his face filled with concern and regret, Kerry saw Nancy begin to move. She struggled to her feet. Her eyes filled with hatred, she grabbed the mallet and lurched toward Donald.

Did Donald see her?

No. He had his back to her. He was still staring intently at Kerry, still explaining, still apologizing.

Donald didn't know she was about to attack him. Only Kerry knew.

Kerry didn't think his numb legs could move. But he had to try. With a desperate effort, he hurtled out of the chair, stumbled forward on aching legs, and threw himself onto Nancy. The mallet flew from her hand. Donald spun around, surprised, and stumbled backward.

"He killed my sister! He killed my sister!" Nancy screamed over and over.

Kerry grabbed Nancy and tried to hold her

still. But she attacked him with her fists, pounding his chest wildly, furiously, screaming and crying. He held her by the shoulders, letting her pound him, until her blows became weak. She uttered a low cry and collapsed to the floor.

"Poor kid," Donald muttered, looking over at her.

His foot throbbing, Kerry hopped back to the wooden chair.

"That was a nice tackle, Ker," Donald said. "Maybe you should try out for defense — you know, tackle or linebacker or something."

"I don't want to talk about football," Kerry groaned.

They heard sirens in the distance. A few seconds later, the cabin was invaded by bright white headlights. The sirens were right outside.

"Here comes the cavalry to the rescue," Donald said.

"You mean — " Kerry started in surprise.

"I called Dad just before I came after you, told him I was headed up here following you. Looks like we're about to have a happy family reunion."

Kerry smiled. He even forgot about his shattered foot for a few seconds.

Donald picked up the moose head and tossed it at Kerry. "Here, Ker, quick — put this back on. Dad has such a dull life. Let's give him a thrill. . . ."

* * *

A few days later, Kerry was heading out of school, struggling with his crutches, his arms aching from pulling and pushing them. He bumped into Sal Murdoch on *his* crutches.

"Copycat," Sal sneered.

"Get a horse," Kerry replied. It wasn't too original, but it got a laugh out of Sal.

"Hey, gimp — over here!" a voice called. It was Josh, gesturing to Kerry on the sidewalk in front of the main entrance. Kerry hurried over to him as best he could, getting his right leg tangled in his right crutch and nearly falling face forward onto the walk. "I thought maybe you could carry my books for me," Josh said.

"Very funny," Kerry growled, kicking at Josh with his good foot.

"Want a lift?"

"Sure," Kerry said.

"Well, don't look at me. You know I don't have a car."

"You're a million laughs today, Josh," Kerry said, leaning on his crutches. "Don't you ever get tired of that joke?"

"Don't you ever get tired of falling for it?"

"Well. . . ."

"Listen, Kerry, I wonder if you could do me a favor. . . ."

"No way," Kerry said, grinning.

"Well . . . my cousin Sarah is coming to town this weekend. She isn't fabulous or anything. But she's a good kid and she's kinda pretty. I think you might like her. I was wondering if maybe you'd like to—"

"I don't *believe* this!" Kerry said, raising a crutch in the air as if to brain Josh with it. "A blind date! Are you seriously suggesting a blind date?"

"Well. . . ." Josh backed away. "I see your point. I guess not. Sorry about that. Uh . . . some other time. Sorry." He turned and started running down the block.

"Hey, wait! Josh!" Kerry propelled himself after Josh, hopping on one leg, raising and lowering the crutches in front of him. "Wait! Not so fast! Let's discuss this. . . . How pretty did you say she was?"

About the Author

R.L. Stine is the author of more than 40 books of humor and adventure for young people, and was formerly an editor of humor magazines at Scholastic. He lives and works in New York City with his wife, Jane, and his son, Matthew. *Blind Date* is his first young adult novel.